Game of Spade's

Written and illustrated by
David Schmidt

CABLE PUBLISHING

Brule, Wisconsin

Game of Spades

First Edition

Published by:

Cable Publishing
14090 E Keinenen Rd
Brule, WI 54820

Website: www.cablepublishing.com
E-mail: nan@cablepublishing.com

This is a work of fiction. Any resemblance to actual people,
living or dead, is purely coincidental.

Soft cover: ISBN 13: 978-1-934980-31-6
                ISBN 10: 1-934980-31-5

Library of Congress Control Number: 2010936990

Printed in the United States of America

THANKS

*This one's for you, Mom...
for loving animals unconditionally
and for always finding a way to make
something out of nothing. – DS*

ORIGIN

A butterfly gently fluttered over a peaceful meadow and landed on a small sapling. Its bright orange and yellow wings silently flapped as it tried to keep its balance on the thin twig.

Chirps from dozens of birds and the occasional chatter of insects were the only sounds that radiated from the quiet valley. A soft wind gingerly blew against the trees and mildly tossed their leaves about. The tall grasses and wildflowers on the forest floor slowly swayed back and forth like waves on the shore of a calm lake.

Suddenly, two small, furry animals burst from the tree line and tumbled in a heap out into the sun.

"Gotcha!" exclaimed the smaller of the two, a gray wolf pup. "Ya can't hide from me! I've got natural hunting and tracking skills!"

"Oh, gimme a break, Mesquite," said the other round ball of fur, a grizzly bear cub. "I stopped playing hide-and-seek when I came across those raspberry bushes. I was on a l-l-lunch break," he stuttered. The little bear liked to eat.

"Sequoia, you lost fair and square and now you're gonna have to find me!" Mesquite quipped.

"I'm tired of this game. Let's g-g-go mess with Aspen instead," the little grizzly offered.

"Okay, loser, since you can't win anyway." Mesquite snipped. "I think she's up on the bluffs. My mom said she saw her this morning."

The two friends started off across the valley toward a large, rocky summit overlooking the meadow.

"Why does she always want to g-g-go up there?" Sequoia asked.

"She likes to pretend she's flying since she's not very good at it," Mesquite said. "Her mom and dad get her up there and show her that peregrine falcons are good flyers and she should be soaring with them by now."

"M-m-maybe she's really not a peregrine falcon at all," Sequoia joked. "Maybe she's a chicken!"

Mesquite burst out laughing at the little bear's comment as they plowed headlong through the long grasses toward the path that led up the cliff.

After the duo had plodded along for nearly an hour, they finally neared the top of the bluff. They could see their little friend, Aspen, out on the edge of a craggy rock. She had her eyes closed and was holding her wings out, pretending to be soaring above the valley. The wind was blowing against her, rustling her feathers

as though she was actually flying.

Mesquite hunkered down so she wouldn't see him. "Hey, Sequoia," he whispered to his friend, "let's sneak up on her and scare her off the cliff! We'll teach her to fly, all right!"

"Not me. You g-g-go ahead. She'll tell her mom and her mom will tell my mom and I'll g-g-get grounded until hibernation time!" the bear replied.

"Fine. I'm not scared. You just sit back and watch an alpha-male wolf in action!" Mesquite said confidently.

He turned away from Sequoia and peered quietly over some blades of grass. He got ready to pounce.

Whack!

Without warning, a small white and blue wing slapped Mesquite across the face and he fell over backward, holding his nose with his front paws.

"Thought you could sneak up on me, huh?" Aspen said proudly, as she tucked her wing back alongside her body. "I heard you a mile away, you idiot!"

"It was his idea!" Mesquite said, pointing his paw at Sequoia.

"Oh, really!" Aspen said, glaring at the bear cub.

"N-n-no it wasn't!" Sequoia stammered. "It wasn't me. He's lying! Mesquite, I'm gonna kick your —"

Suddenly, the roar of a private jet cut off the adolescent grizzly. It cruised low and fast and blasted by

them with a horrendous shudder. It was a stealthy, high-tech aircraft — shiny black in color, but with bright red symbols on the sides. It was making a high-speed getaway back to its home base after a secret and successful mission of arson.

"What was that?!" Aspen exclaimed. "How rude!"

The three friends shook the dust off and looked in the direction of the jet. It was already out of sight.

Sequoia stuck his nose up and smelled the air in the jet's wake. "Do you smell smoke?" he asked.

Mesquite and Aspen joined their friend in sniffing the air. The normally fresh, clean air of the valley was mixing heavily with the scent of burning wood.

"You're right," Mesquite said. "The forest is on fire!"

The trio bounded over to the other side of the bluff from where the jet had first appeared for a better look at the valley below.

What they saw shocked them. A wild, ferocious fire was rapidly consuming the forest below. Orange and red flames ripped at the trees and grasses as clouds of thick, grayish-black smoke poured upward into the sky. The fire was accelerating and encircling the entire valley. It looked as though it would consume everything.

"We gotta get home!" the three friends exclaimed at practically the same time.

Aspen leaped off the cliff, flapping her little wings

fiercely as she struggled to fly. "I'll check the way!" she yelled to the wolf and bear younglings as they hustled down the path to the valley below.

The artificially inspired fire raged and very quickly devoured everything in its path. It swarmed over the valley like a fiery flood.

In a panic, Mesquite and Sequoia scrambled down the trail. Terrified, they were trying to get back to their dens where their families were surely waiting for them. As they rounded a corner near the end of the trail, they encountered Aspen on a tree limb overlooking the path.

"We can't go this way!" she shouted as she tried to catch her breath. Her wings were tired from flying just a short distance. "We have to go around to the east," she said, pointing with her wing. "If we can get over the river, we can catch up with our families from the other side. I won't be able to fly much more. We have to hurry!"

The boys nodded and headed off through the brush and around the hillside. It was slow going since there was no trail and neither of them had ever gone that way before. They were all scared.

The sky was blackening and all the smoke was blotting out the sun. It started to look like dusk even though it was a sunny afternoon. Everything had a dark orange, hazy look to it. The hoarse rumbling sounds

of the fire made it hard to hear. The swirling winds generated by the flames carried an amazing amount of gray ash, making it look almost as if it were snowing.

The three animals finally got to the far side of the hill only to find the valley that faced them already submitting to the power of the flames.

"We've got to go back!" Mesquite shouted, and he started to turn around.

The fire was overrunning the forest behind them. Trees, still aflame, toppled in the forest and crashed to the ground. The fire had surrounded them.

"There's only one way out!" Sequoia yelled above the noise and confusion. "We have to jump in the river and let it carry us out of here! Aspen, you can ride on me down the stream — I know you can't swim."

"Let's do it!" Mesquite plunged into the river and was immediately swept away by its torrent. Sequoia followed him in without hesitating. Aspen flew down and landed on the cub's back as Sequoia frantically tried to paddle for control.

The river rushed them along through the burning forest. They passed safely through intense patches of heat and thick black smoke. Flames leaped out from all directions but never touched the hapless trio as they whirled about in the rushing waters. Burning embers fell about them, extinguishing with a loud hiss as they hit the water.

After a while, the burning forest slowly disappeared behind them. The air grew cleaner and the sky was clearer as the river snaked its way down through a ravine.

The river was running faster and faster, and they soon found themselves at risk of being drowned instead of burned alive.

Mesquite and Sequoia were almost exhausted from swimming so hard. Aspen was doing all she could to hang on. Her little talons gripped the fur of her young grizzly friend as tightly as possible.

A short distance ahead, Mesquite could see the river becoming very rough, with jutting boulders and dangerous fast-moving water. The drenched little wolf pup turned to his friends splashing violently behind him.

"We've got to get out of the river!" he shouted. "There's a dead tree up ahead hanging over the water. Grab onto it and pull yourselves out!"

The trio slammed into the fallen tree but managed to hang on with their claws as the rushing river pulled at them. Aspen had just enough energy left to fly onto the log and she shouted desperately for her friends to get out of the river.

Mesquite managed to get out first and, after getting a firm grip, he bent over and grabbed onto Sequoia with his teeth. He tugged and tugged until the soaked bear got a foothold on a branch and hoisted himself out of the raging waters.

They stumbled off the tree and collapsed onto a thin strip of ground. Panting heavily and trying to catch their breath, they could see that they were at the base of a rocky wall next to the river.

After a few minutes of lying there, trying to regain their strength, they were startled by a cry for help from the river. They bolted upright and peered over the riverbank. Swimming frantically just upstream, a small, lanky animal was helplessly heading for the rapids.

"W-w-we got to save her!" Sequoia bellowed. He sprang on the fallen tree and held his paw down into the water to try to rescue the distressed creature caught in the river's current.

As she came by, she latched onto the grizzly cub's thick paw. Sequoia lifted her easily out of the water and onto the relative safety of the tree limb. The wiry animal shook the water off herself and scampered to solid ground. The others could now clearly see that she was a young black-footed ferret.

"Oh, thank you, thank you. You saved my life!" she said to Sequoia as he joined them on the riverbank. "My name is Juniper. What's yours?"

The grizzly bear, gray wolf and peregrine falcon younglings introduced themselves to their new friend as wisps of smoke and ash swirled all around. The fire was darkening the sky above them. It was getting closer.

"C'mon," Mesquite said. "We've gotta keep moving. The wind's blowing the fire this way. We'll have to walk from here."

The exhausted quartet got to their feet and headed away from the approaching wildfire. The raging river was to one side of them, the rocky cliff to the other, and the fire was quickly approaching from the rear.

They didn't get more than a few dozen steps before their thin pathway stopped abruptly at the top of a sheer drop-off to the rapids below.

Aspen flew up onto Sequoia's shoulders to peer over the edge. "End of the road, guys," she said. "What are we going to do now?"

The animals looked around and at each other. Things had gotten pretty grim.

Just then, they heard a voice from the craggy rock face above. "Up here! Climb up! You'll be safe up here!" It was a badger cub calling down to them from a ledge.

The animals were relieved, but knew they couldn't scale the rocks to get to him.

"How do we get up there? It's too steep!" Juniper shouted up to him as she stood up on her back feet.

"There's sort of a path back that way a bit," the badger yelled down to them while pointing with his paw. "It's not easy, but you should be able to make it. You better hurry!"

The group wasted no time and a few minutes later, after clambering up the rocks, they came face to face with the little badger high above the river.

"C'mon," their rescuer said. "There's a cave back this way. We'll be safe there."

"Thanks, friend," Sequoia said. "What's y-y-your name?"

"Cedar," he said.

"Well, Cedar, I'm Sequoia," the bear said. "This is Aspen, that's Mesquite and she's Juniper."

"That's quite a wildfire," Cedar said as he glanced over his shoulder. "We should all consider ourselves lucky. Like you guys, I barely escaped getting cooked back there. Fortunately, I came across this cave."

The group walked around a large boulder at the mouth of the cave. Cedar led them into the cool, dark opening and along a thin, sandy trail down deep inside the underground cavity. They eventually came to a larger open area where they all could sit and rest. In a few hours, the firestorm should harmlessly pass them by.

It took a moment for all of them to finally relax a little and dwell mournfully on the tragic events of the day. They were orphaned animals now.

Without warning, a man emerged out of the shadows of the cave. It was an elderly tribal chief. He wore a glorious headdress of feathers and beads. His clothes

were made of buckskin, as were the moccasins on his feet. The old chief held a very old and oddly shaped walking stick. He made absolutely no sound when he moved and as he stepped forward, his feet never quite touched the ground. He seemed to be somewhat transparent.

The animals were startled by his presence. They jumped back and gathered tightly together on the other side of the cave.

"Do not be frightened," he said. "This is my home; I am the great chief of the shamans of the tribes of the four winds. You are my guests, and I have been expecting you for a very long time. You have been brought here to be together, for the five of you are truly one."

The badger decided that he had had enough of this stranger and his strange ways. He stepped forward a little and bared his teeth, hoping to scare the ghost-man away.

"I mean you no harm, Cedar," the Native American said. The ancient man could tell that they feared him.

Cedar backed down.

"Oh," the chief said as he chuckled a little. "I see you are shocked that I know your names. I know all of you and, believe it or not, all of you know me — at least in your hearts."

The animals looked at each other, puzzled. This was

truly a day of amazing events.

"We speak the same language, you and I. Your ancestors taught us the ways of nature…the circle of life. They taught us to dance, to sing and to laugh. And they also taught us to fight and survive," the old spirit said. "And, now, it is time to fight again."

The tribal chief sat down, his legs crossed beneath him. He still did not touch the ground; instead he mysteriously hovered several inches above it.

"Gather around me, my brothers and sisters," the Native American said as he spread out his arms. "Much has been taken from you this day…but much is about to be given. You are a family now. Stay together, for you will be the law of the land."

The animals approached the spirit-chief, no longer afraid of him. They sat in a semicircle in front of him and listened intently.

The shaman waved his walking stick across the ground in front of them, and a small, bright-blue flame snaked up from under the sand and stones of the cave floor. It danced and flickered, finally growing into a small, mystical campfire. The flames generated no heat, only a metaphysical, turquoise-colored light that bounced off the cave walls all around them.

"The earth has been dishonored too many times, my friends. She is bountiful, but she can take no more. The

evil that has come over this land must be stopped. You five have been chosen to be her guardians," the elder revealed.

The animals heard ancient Native American drums and chants from invisible people echo throughout the cavern. The sounds grew louder and louder, but the old chief was the only one there with them. The blue-green blaze on the cave floor burned brighter.

"Now reach into the fire, my brothers and sisters. Remove a stone from the enchanted flames," he said.

The animals, eyes open wide in wonderment, hesitantly leaned into the magical blaze and each pulled out a small, flat stone. The strange turquoise fire did not burn at all, but tickled their skin. The five creatures of the forest sat back, looking down at the glowing gems in their grasp.

"Now turn them over, and you will see that each stone is marked with your imprint," said the spirit chief. The animals did as they were told and noticed their footprints had pressed into the rock on the other side.

"These are the source of your power; you must keep them with you at all times," he continued. "It is told that turquoise has healing and protective powers. It promotes spiritual harmony and dispels negative energy and impurity. You have been granted great responsibility and great authority. The spirits of the entire first

nations are behind you, and the fate of mother earth is before you."

The shaman reached into a satchel tied to his belt and pulled out five long, leather cords. He went to each animal, tied a cord to their amulet stones, and placed them around their necks like a pendant. He then stepped back behind the flickering fire and smiled at his animal audience.

"When you are in danger," he said as they looked up at him in amazement, "the amulets will bring the spirits of your animal and native warrior ancestors into your hearts. You will become more powerful than you can imagine. It is your destiny to right the wrongs of the land and bring balance back to the planet. You only have to believe...."

Suddenly, the blue-green fire separated into five distinct flames and shot straight into each animal's amulet. The necklaces glowed brightly with an intense neon-blue color that swirled about the five little animals like a tornado made of pure light.

Then, with one last powerfully brilliant flash, each animal transformed into his or her powerful, noble alter-ego. They raised up on their hind legs, human-like, in a proud, heroic stance with their heads held high and their chests jutting forward.

Mesquite transformed into a large, valiant humanoid

wolf with incredible fighting skills, armed with a long wooden staff with an enchanted spear tip that he could summon at will.

Aspen became a regal falcon-woman, her wings tipped with mystical feathers that she could shoot like missiles with deadly accuracy and power.

Sequoia morphed into a massive, muscular, fully grown man-like grizzly with a huge, unbreakable magical shield grasped in his left arm.

Cedar grew into a stocky, brawny man-sized badger with claws that could carve through steel and tunnel him at incredible speeds behind enemy lines.

Finally, Juniper changed into an ultra-athletic and extremely flexible ferret-woman blessed with super-speed. Whenever she transformed, a leather pack automatically appeared on her back that was filled with small wooden handles that she could magically turn into hatchets with just her touch.

The Natural Forces heroes looked at each other and felt their newly found power course through their superhuman bodies. Together, they felt unstoppable.

Without another word, the shaman chief had disappeared back into the shadows from which he came, bound for his home in the spirit realm.

Their adventures were about to begin and the world would never be the same.

CHAPTER 1

Nathan Axxes, chief executive officer and president of the Axxes Conglomeration, was sitting in his oversized office on the top floor of his headquarters building at his massive desk custom-made from a thousand-year-old redwood tree. He was talking on the phone.

His corporate attorney, Miranda Wright, was sitting against the wall on an overstuffed calfskin leather sofa. A strikingly beautiful woman with a seductive aura, Miranda had long, jet-black hair and a tall, athletic body.

She was born blind, without pupils, in a bayou of Louisiana not far from Baton Rouge. Miranda's olive-colored skin gives away her Portuguese ancestry, but her heritage is completely Creole. Her parents sacrificed everything in order to restore their daughter's vision but modern medicine could do nothing for her. So they brokered a deal with a voodoo swamp priestess and through the use of forbidden witchcraft she was given the power of a remarkable hypnotic gaze that she uses in and out of court to win people over to her unscrupulous way of thinking.

"Has it been arranged?" Axxes said to the person on the other end of the phone. "I want this to go smoothly. Make sure you bring the specially bottled water I sent you. Make sure the driver drinks it."

Nathan Axxes is a wiry older man with pale skin and spindly, elongated fingers. His long, silvery hair cascades down past his shoulders like fine silk. He is slender and tall, imposing and ominous. One of the wealthiest men on the planet, his desire for more wealth and power never tires and he stops at nothing to ensure he gets results.

The Axxes corporation he inherited many years ago is a global company specializing in seizing the earth's resources and selling them at a huge profit. Mining, drilling, cutting and clearing - no job is too big or too small for Axxes. He is also a land baron, arms dealer, and he spends billions on research and development of diabolical designs.

After a slight pause, Nathan continued his telephonic conversation. "This little accident is critical to our plans, Mr. Spade. With this spill, we can shut down the roads in and out of the park and use that time to set our systems in place. We need those rigs linked up and at the spot that I indicated on the map we sent you before the authorities get there. There is little room for mistakes,

Spade. Do I make myself clear?"

He got the answer he wanted and a villainous grin crept across his vampire-like face.

"Good. Remember, it must appear to be an accident. When you get there, call the number I gave you. And then hand the phone to the driver. Tell him I want to talk to him personally." Axxes snickered and hung up the phone.

He looked at Miranda and smiled. She detected his pleasure and grinned in return at her boss with a cynical expression. Their evil plot was off to a good start.

*****

On a desolate forest access road in the western-most part of Rocky Mountain National Park, just a few miles north of the town of Grand Lake, Colorado, a scrawny man dressed in khaki overalls stood next to a large truck. Obscured from view, its open bay was loaded with large yellow barrels crafted of a peculiar plastic material. Hazardous waste decals were stuck all over them.

The truck driver watched as a shiny black Hummer with oversized tires sped down the 4x4 trail and screeched to a halt in front of him. It kicked up a sizable

amount of dust that caused the driver to cough and wipe his eyes.

The Hummer doors were adorned with the logo of the Axxes Conglomeration. As the driver of the vehicle opened the door and hoisted himself out, he crushed a wildflower growing on the side of the road under his steel-toed work boot. The frail trucker started fidgeting nervously; his boss had arrived and he was not friendly.

Burt Spade is the Director of Field Operations for the Axxes Conglomeration, a position in which he serves with great enthusiasm. Spade, a huge man and dedicated employee, lost his right arm in an explosion several years ago while detonating dynamite in a coal mine owned by Axxes.

After the accident, Nathan Axxes personally supervised his company's Research and Development Medical Experimentation Team as they worked to create a variety of interchangeable mechanical arms to replace the one Burt had lost. Spade, overwhelmed by the newfound power his artificial limb gave him, knew that he owed his very existence to Mr. Axxes and would do anything for him or his company. The mechanical appendages cost millions of dollars – Spade vowed to work for the company to repay his debt or until the day he died, whichever comes first.

Spade's new right arms serve additional duty as field tools; whether as a massive drill, jackhammer, flame-thrower, forklift or a variety of other types. He keeps his spare arms in the back of his Hummer for easy access.

On this calm, autumn day, Spade was wearing his prosthetic limb with a formidable claw-like device on the end, which helped him hold the steering wheel. The jittery worker noticed that his supervisor's massive mechanical talon was clenching a small cooler as he approached.

"Is everything ready?" Spade growled to the worker. The worker, too scared to speak to the monstrous man towering over him, nodded in agreement.

"Good," Spade replied. "I brought you some water. You gotta hydrate in these mountains, you know. The elevation will just kill ya if you're not careful."

Spade opened up the little red cooler, pulled a plastic water bottle out its icy resting place and tossed it at the truck driver. The timid man bobbled the catch, but managed to not completely embarrass himself by dropping it to the ground.

"Drink up!" Spade bellowed and looked the little fellow directly in the eyes to ensure he obeyed his order.

The courier cracked the plastic top and took a big swig. It was refreshing. This was the first time the man

could recall ever seeing Burt Spade do something thoughtful.

"Thank you, sir," the man said with an unsure smile and then downed another long gulp of the cold water.

Spade ignored him and walked around the truck to look at the barrels stuffed in the back. With his left arm, he reached in and pushed on them. They were fastened securely in the truck's bed by thick straps and locked in place by a network of chains. Spade reached in with his replacement arm and, using his steel claw, snapped the chains and cut through the straps in a matter of seconds.

Then he came full circle around the truck and walked up to the minuscule driver like a bully about to take away a smaller child's milk money. "Perfect. Ya done good," the monster of a man said. "The cargo looks secure," he continued with a wicked smile full of crooked teeth. "You're gonna make me proud, Daniel."

"Ah, it's actually Donald, sir," the driver said cautiously. "My name's Donald."

Spade sneered back at the smaller man, shocked that he dared correct him. It would have been better if the man just changed his name to Daniel. "Yeah, whatever," Burt replied. "This is an important mission. No room for mistakes."

Donald was confused. "Uh, I don't understand, sir," he said with a shaky voice that he tried to calm with another swig from his water bottle. "The manifest said this is a shipment of highly-concentrated insecticide. I'm just delivering these barrels to the Estes Park Ranger Station, on the other side of the continental divide, right?"

Spade's smile barely hid the truth inside. "Yeah, that's right. But if anything happens to your cargo, well, something terrible could happen. You got a lot of toxic chemicals back there. I need a driver I can count on."

"Oh, you can count on me, Mr. Spade," Donald tried to assure him. "I haven't been with the company very long and I know you guys prefer your own hand-built workforce, but I won't let you down." As if to seal his statement with authority, he gulped down the last of the water Spade had given him and threw the empty container in the truck.

"Now that's my boy," Spade said. "You know, I almost forgot… Nathan Axxes himself wanted to send you off with some kind words. Let me dial him on my cell and you can talk to him yourself."

The short transporter's eyes opened wide with surprise and anticipation. "Really? Mr. Axxes wants to talk to me?"

Spade was already dialing the phone as Donald beamed with delight and rubbed his hands together excitedly.

"It's ringing," Burt told Donald and held up his left index finger to indicate it shouldn't be long. "Uh, hello, Mr. Axxes? This is Burt Spade, sir. You asked me to call you once we were ready. I got Daniel here who's gonna be driving the truck."

After a brief pause, Spade handed the phone to Donald, whose face looked like a child's on Christmas morning.

A high-pitched digital squeal came across the line as Donald held the phone to his ear. His eyes suddenly turned gray as his pupils shrank and a zombie-like expression fell across his face. He was in a trance.

After a few seconds, Spade grabbed the phone from Donald's hand and shoved the hapless man inside the cab of the truck. In a robotic state, Donald sat there stiff and motionless.

Spade quickly dropped to the ground and crawled under the front of the truck. With his claw, he reached up and ripped out the brake lines. Red brake fluid dripped profusely to the ground below.

Then Spade pulled himself back out and stood up. He walked over to the driver's door of the truck and

leaned inside just enough to be sure the hypnotized driver could hear him.

"Time to drive, little man!" Spade decreed.

Donald fired up the big truck and put it in gear. Without delay, he slowly drove down the forest road a little ways and pulled out onto Highway 34. He hadn't blinked in nearly five minutes.

CHAPTER 2

Gathered in their juvenile forms, the five animal friends that make up the Natural Forces found themselves in awe of the alpine wilderness they were walking through.

Flanked by majestic mountains, sixty of them with peaks over 12,000 feet high, and surrounded by lush valleys and cold rushing streams, it is truly an animal's paradise. Except for the winter months.

The air was thinner than the fivesome was used to, but they adjusted rather quickly and hardly noticed it when the scenery offered so much. It was early summer and Rocky Mountain National Park was revealing itself in its full glory.

They were in the southwestern part of the park, not far from the charming town of Grand Lake that sits on the northern edge of the lake from which it gets its namesake. They had snuck down there in the morning hours and scavenged up their morning meal.

Walking in single file, with Mesquite the wolf pup in front as usual, the youngsters were having a great time. They had wandered back up into the safety of the

park and were admiring the view.

Suddenly, Mesquite looked at the ground and stopped. The other kids ambling along behind him were not paying attention and they ran into each other in rapid succession like a slow-moving, furry train.

"What is it?" The badger cub said as he shook his head after colliding with Sequoia's rump.

"Shhh! Cedar, be quiet!" Mesquite shot back.

Mesquite sniffed at the ground and then at the air with his sensitive canine snout. He developed a concerned look and glanced around toward his four animal friends.

"Something's fishy!" he said with an exaggerated and troubled voice.

Mesquite smelled at the ground again. He slowly raised his head, smelling the area around them.

"What is it?" Juniper, the youthful black-footed ferret, asked, insistent and worried.

Mesquite looked back at the ground for a moment and then his concentration broke. He grinned wildly as turned to look at his four pals clinging to his every word.

"It's Sequoia's breath!" Mesquite burst out, jokingly. The little wolf was always into mischief and loved to frolic. His best friend, the bear cub, was his favorite target.

Sequoia frowned and glared at the prankster while the others laughed and giggled.

"Ha, ha, very funny," the little bear said. "Laugh it up."

Cedar couldn't help but continue snickering at their friend who was the brunt of the joke. After all, Sequoia did find a half-eaten trout in the dumpster this morning.

"Be q-q-quiet, you!" Sequoia hollered to the little badger who was erupting in hysterics.

The foursome only started laughing louder. Sequoia, visibly upset, leaped at the group of giggling animal kids. A harmless tussle ensued and the animals wound up in a rolling, raucous pile - a variety of furry legs protruding from the pile.

Aspen flew up to a branch a few feet away to avoid the childish ruckus. She was always bothered by the constant antics of the others and felt too aloof to act so immature.

"You behave like a bunch of idiots," the peregrine falcon, barely out of the nest, said to the group rolling around in the wild grass.

Suddenly, their playful party was abruptly interrupted by the sound of screeching tires and smashing metal from a nearby road.

The furry foursome stopped wrestling and listened to the sound. Something terrible was happening.

They untangled themselves and ran to the edge of a nearby bluff. The youngsters peered across the small meadow below to see that a truck carrying a load of yellow barrels had sideswiped a car and was careening out of control. Glancing further down the road, they realized that the truck was fast approaching a sharp bend in the road and the driver had lost all control. A horrific crash was less than a minute away and no doubt whatever was in those barrels was going to spill everywhere and into the river just a few hundred yards ahead.

"C'mon, guys!" Mesquite barked. "We gotta stop that truck!"

He jumped up and with a brilliant flash of turquoise light, instantly transformed into his adult alter ego. The others followed suit, but before Sequoia could change into his massive grizzly bear persona, Mesquite held up his hand to stop him.

"Hold it, Sequoia!" Mesquite ordered, clearly in charge and with a plan in mind already. "I need you to stay small for a minute." Then he turned toward the others.

"Cedar, get down there and take out the tires! That should slow the truck down. Juniper, you're the fastest — see if the driver's all right! Aspen, fly Sequoia down

there and drop him in front where he can do some real good," Mesquite finished.

Sequoia realized what the plan was and flashed a self-satisfied grin.

Cedar reared back his arms, brandished his formidable claws that were radiating with bright blue energy and tore into the ground. In seconds, he was tunneling toward the truck at incredible speed.

Juniper bolted after the truck in a blur — a blue-green streak that rushed across the valley.

Aspen quickly flew up to tree level, swerved and swooped down to grab Sequoia gently in her talons. She whisked him up and, with a few rapid flaps of her mighty wings, sped off in the direction of the truck with the little bear grasped firmly in her feet.

"Just d-d-don't drop me!" he shouted with alarm up to Aspen. Sequoia, who always stuttered when he was nervous, had bravery by the ton once he transformed into his super-self.

Mesquite ran to the edge of the bluff and leapt into the air. His momentum carried him far and he rolled as he landed, sprang back to his feet and continued on a high-speed intercept course with the truck.

Juniper, now four-feet-tall and humanistic, reached the truck far ahead of the others. The lightning-fast

ferret jumped up into the cab of the runaway truck through the driver's open window and realized he was non-responsive. She shook him in an effort to wake him, but he was transfixed by something unnatural.

Juniper looked back over the truck's dashboard at the road ahead. The dangerous curve was closing fast. She tried to pry the driver's hands off the steering wheel but she just wasn't strong enough so she jumped on the brake pedal but to no avail. She hopped into the passenger's seat just in time to see Mesquite appear in the road ahead.

Juniper stuck her head out the window and yelled to him. "Mesquite! It won't stop!"

Mesquite looked up and assessed the situation. He could see that the driver of the truck was paralyzed by something. He glanced to the sky and saw Aspen swooping in with Sequoia in tow. He hoped they would make it in time.

All of a sudden, Cedar burst through the asphalt a few feet in front of Mesquite. The truck was headed straight at him.

Cedar flattened to the road as the truck bore down on him — it passed directly overhead and as it did, he reached out with his powerful arms and slashed all the tires with his razor-sharp claws. The tires ripped apart

under his assault and chunks of rubber spewed out across the road behind the wayward vehicle. Cedar spun around when he emerged from the rear of the truck to see if his attack was enough.

The truck lurched and slowed but still wasn't stopping. It had too much weight behind it and had built up too much momentum from the hill it was on. It headed straight for Mesquite and would surely crash through the small guardrail at the edge of the turn.

Mesquite gritted his teeth and jumped at the side of the truck as it sped past. He threw open the door, broke the driver's firm grip from the steering wheel and pulled him out of the broken rig. Mesquite landed safely on the side of the road with the clueless truck driver cradled in his arms.

Juniper abandoned the truck as well and latched onto an overhanging tree limb as it passed by. She steadied herself and watched the out-of-control truck skid ever forward.

Aspen zoomed in overhead and released Sequoia while still in flight like some sort of brown-haired bomb. "Okay, big guy, it's up to you now!" she screamed to her small friend as he fell toward the highway.

Sequoia morphed into his massive grizzly bear adult form on his way to the ground and landed with a solid,

heavy thud. His huge, clawed feet broke open the pavement as he touched down. Turning, he saw the truck rumbling directly at him. A determined look came over his face and he clenched his teeth to ready himself for the hit.

Unswerving, he held out his mighty arms and leaned forward, stiffening his muscles for the impact. The truck lurched violently as it slammed into the huge grizzly-man. Sequoia's oversized hands made two massive dents and the entire front of the truck crumpled as he struggled to stop it.

The barrels in the back jostled vigorously about from the sudden jolt, one of them somersaulting off the flatbed and crashing down into the brush by the side of the road.

The truck kept pushing Sequoia backwards. His great strength was slowing the big rig, but not completely stopping it. The big bruin pushed even harder, his feet plowing deep furrows in the road as the truck shoved him back.

Sequoia's back muscles rippled under his heavy coat of fur as he strained with all his strength. He dug his heels in harder and roared from the exertion. The truck groaned as its steel frame buckled, and finally it came to a stop at the very edge of the curve in the road.

Sequoia relaxed his fatigued muscles and looked behind him at the valley below. His hind quarters were actually touching the guardrail. He exhaled and wiped his sweaty brow with the back of his forearm.

Mesquite and the others ran up to the exhausted grizzly still in front of the wreckage. They were constantly astonished at his feats of strength.

"That was a close one!" Mesquite said, relieved.

"Tell me about it," Sequoia replied, his stuttering completely gone. "How's the driver?"

"I think he's in a coma or something," Juniper said. "I don't know what happened to him, but he'll be all right, I think."

Aspen landed next to her teammates. "I saw flashing lights coming this way. Police and ambulance, no doubt. Let's scramble before somebody sees us," she implored.

The five friends rushed back into the forest, leaving the crippled truck at the end of the road and the driver in the shade of a large pine tree.

CHAPTER
3

From his headquarters in Los Angeles, Nathan Axxes was monitoring the mission in Colorado by Internet, television and secretly hacking into the emergency communications network of Larimer and Grand counties in which the Rocky Mountain National Park resides. He was instantly aware that the concocted accident didn't quite go as planned.

Raging with anger, he dialed Burt Spade on his secure phone.

"Spade, you blundering idiot," Axxes seethed into the phone, "you have exactly two minutes to explain to me how you botched such a simple task!"

Burt, who was not far from the park entrance, was baffled. He wasn't aware that the truck never crashed and the yellow barrels never spilled. "Sir?" he asked. "I don't understand. There are sirens going off and they even shut down the road getting into the park. What's the matter?"

Axxes was eager to enlighten his underling. "I'm listening to the police channels, you moron, like you're supposed to be doing. Besides hitting a sedan with a

family of four inside, the truck never crashed at all. It didn't flip and they're reporting that the barrels are still in the back."

"But, Mr. Axxes," Spade stammered, "I did everything like you asked. The driver drank the water and I sent him on his way."

Nathan had little patience and even less sympathy. "Get your fat butt over there, you miserable dolt! That truck belongs to us, and the driver is an employee of the company. We're going to have investigators crawling down our throats."

Axxes paused for a minute as he listened to more transmissions on the police radios 1,000 miles away.

"The cops are saying the truck's tires blew out and it may have hit a moose or something," Axxes relayed. "The driver was apparently ejected but is unharmed besides being in a state of shock and non-responsive. He's already in an ambulance and on the way to the nearest hospital. They say that all twelve barrels on the truck are fine."

Spade was busily trying to tune in his police band radio while talking to his employer at the same time. He was agitated and nervous. "What was that, sir? Did you say they're reporting twelve barrels?"

"Yes, " the villainous boss shot back. "Twelve."

Burt recognized an opportunity to salvage their twisted plan. "But, Mr. Axxes, sir, I counted thirteen barrels in the back. There's one missing."

"You better be right, Spade," warned Nathan. "Maybe we got lucky and one of them bounced out. Did you make sure the tops were not sealed when they were loaded yesterday like I asked?"

Burt knew he hadn't forgotten to do that part. "Yes, sir!" he exclaimed. "They're loose and ready to pop open with the slightest bump."

"Good," Axxes said, calming down a bit. "We might just rescue this mission yet."

He vile mind had already devised a way to continue with his scheme. Axxes spit out his orders to Spade, "Get to the scene of the accident. Tell those badge-wearing simpletons that one of the barrels is missing and contains extremely dangerous and toxic chemicals. Tell them we are prepared for such a contingency and that we have a team on standby to contain the spill.

"They'll go by their standard playbook and shut the area down. Nobody in or out. Then, just like the original plan, we'll send in our own hazardous materials clean-up crew and, at the same time, sneak in our biotech production equipment and install them at the hidden location along the river."

Spade was glad that he hadn't botched the assignment. "Won't word get out about the spill? What about the press and the environmental scumbags?"

"That is why I'm the brains and you're the muscle, my oafish friend," Nathan gloated as he leaned back in his chair. "I've already accounted for that in our original plan, which would have been a much worse spill.

"This is peak season for tourism in that overrated national park. With just a little coercing from Miranda here, the government will cover up what happened rather than risk losing millions in tourism to their beloved park. They will never admit that their number one contractor handling the Mountain Pine Beetle infestation that is destroying their precious forests dumped untold gallons of poisonous insecticide into the water system.

"We'll have them close the park for miles on each side and claim that the road needs extensive repair. That should give us enough time to set up our secret little factory right under their noses.

"Now then, Burt my boy, do you think your puny brain can handle this and get the plan back on track?"

"Yes, sir," Burt quickly replied. "I got this."

"You better, Spade," Axxes forewarned him, "or I'll see to it that all your arms are melted into slag and

you'll be using a broomstick for a limb the rest of your pathetic life." Nathan slammed the receiver back into its cradle and turned to Miranda, who was perched on the corner of his desk.

"My dear," Axxes said, his tone completely congenial, "I need you to handle the nuances of this operation and ensure all the loose ends are taken care of."

Miranda smiled. She seemed to almost relish the fact that Spade had made a mess of things. She despised him and his bullying, overly aggressive ways, preferring her own techniques of persuasion, devious influence, and merciless application of the martial arts.

"It would be my pleasure, Nathan," she said. "I will leave first thing tomorrow."

"Oh, and one more thing," Mr. Axxes added. "If Spade loses control of this, if the millions of dollars I've spent working on this plan are threatened in any way or if it appears we are going to be found out, I need you to fix it and erase those responsible."

Ms. Wright liked the sound of that. "Of course, sir. Nothing will go wrong," she assured him. "What could possibly stand in our way?"

Not far from the final resting place of the totaled truck, the Natural Forces team, regressed back into their adolescent forms, gathered together in a thicket of aspen trees. They were watching the flurry of activity as the local police, ambulance and a few park rangers scurried about trying to assess the situation. They were jabbering on their radios while a couple of them took some photos with their digital cameras. They seemed particularly fascinated by the long ditches that Sequoia's heels ripped into the blacktop as he tried to stop the truck.

"Did any of you guys get a good look at the barrels that truck was hauling?" Mesquite asked. "I think I saw one of them go flying off the back."

"Not me," Juniper said.

"Me neither," Sequoia said sarcastically. "All I s-s-saw was a g-g-great big grille of a g-g-great big truck."

Aspen stepped forward. "I had a great view from above of the whole thing," she stated. "And one of those barrels did bounce off the truck when our stuttering friend here got up close and personal with it. It

rolled pretty far. It's somewhere over there in the tall marsh grass." She pointed with her little wing to a spot about 50 yards from where they were now.

"I'm curious what's in it," Mesquite mentioned. "If it's something nasty, maybe we should help the humans find it so they can take care of it."

"Well, nobody knows it's there since we were the only ones to witness the whole thing," Aspen said. "I hate to say it, but Mesquite's right."

Cedar wasn't anxious to go anywhere near it. "Not me. You guys go right ahead. That barrel is probably full of nuclear waste and it's probably all over the place by now. You're all going to end up glowing in the dark and puking your guts out."

"All the more reason to alert the humans, don't you think?" Mesquite emphasized. "We should do the right thing."

"I agree," Juniper joined in.

"C'mon, Cedar," Sequoia pleaded. "I thought you were a tough guy."

"Keep pushing me, cub," Cedar snipped, "and you'll find out just how tough I can be."

Aspen took to wing while the others plodded over cautiously in the direction of the missing barrel — even Cedar, who made sure to be the last in their little formation.

Aspen, flying rather gracelessly over the site, spotted it first. "Over here!" she yelled back to the others. "It's over here!"

Then she landed on a dead limb of a nearby evergreen that had been ravaged from the inside out by a bevy of pine beetles the year before. It was just one of millions of dead lodgepole pines in the mountains that now outnumber the healthy green ones. Their reddish-gray wooden skeletons cover the landscape as far as the eye can see.

The bright yellow container that sprang from the truck bed lay at the bottom of a small grass-covered ravine in a dense strand of cattails. From the road, it was practically impossible to see.

The mammals approached the barrel with extreme caution, sniffing the air and the ground as they tried to detect anything unusual. They noticed danger and caution warnings were written clearly all over it and some rather brightly colored decals of scientific symbols as well as a skull-and-crossbones.

Mesquite inched ever closer, trying to be brave in front of the others but also taking heed in Cedar's earlier warning. He most certainly didn't want to irradiate himself.

"It looks like the top is nearly off," the young wolf

said. "But it doesn't look like anything's spilled out."

Sequoia plodded down next to his friend and thrust his snout toward the barrel. His amazing sense of smell should easily identify something out of the ordinary.

"Smells OK," the infant grizzly said.

"I say we try to push the top back on better and then try to roll it closer to the road so the humans see it and pick it up," Mesquite proposed.

"You're crazy," Cedar shouted from his spot a safe distance away. "I ain't touching that thing!"

"Stop being such a wuss," Mesquite hollered back. "It's going to take all of us to move this thing!"

Juniper spoke up; she was starting to believe in Cedar's philosophy. "I don't think this is such a good idea, you guys."

"I agree with the ferret," Aspen asserted from her perch above them all.

"Oh, for crying out loud!" Mesquite angrily proclaimed. He pulled back from the barrel and walked over to where Aspen, Juniper and Cedar were mustered. "You guys are nothing but a bunch of wimpy chickens! I am so tired of having to lead you all..."

Cedar immediately interrupted him, "Whoa! What makes you think that you are the leader? I don't recall voting you in charge."

"Yeah, Mesquite," Aspen vented, "just because you always run to get up in front of us doesn't mean you're the leader!"

"This is unbelievable!" Mesquite said. "Let me explain to you about what an alpha wolf is; you see, in nature…"

"Oh, geez, not this again!" Juniper moaned while Mesquite droned on about his justification for taking on a leadership role.

"Uh, guys," Aspen said loudly, breaking into the conversation. "Guys, is Sequoia doing what I think he's doing?"

The three others turned their attention to where Aspen was already staring in awe. Sequoia had managed to pop off the lid of the barrel and was lapping up its contents like a thirsty dog. His stubby tail was wagging happily from the tip of his rotund rump.

"Aaah!" Juniper cried out. "Sequoia, you idiot! What are you doing?"

From inside the barrel, Sequoia's head emerged. He looked to see what Juniper was screaming about. Liquid dripped from his muzzle.

"What's the problem? It's only w-w-water," he said, matter-of-factly.

The animals were horrified and just stood there,

staring at their friend. He stared back at them and then blinked.

"Want some?" he asked. "It's pretty good."

The foursome turned and looked at each other, puzzled. Either their stupid friend was about to die right in front of them or he was actually right and the container was filled with water.

Without saying a word, they waited a few moments. Minutes ticked by until finally Mesquite broke the awkward silence, "You sure that's only water?"

Aspen joined in, "Sequoia, are you feeling alright?"

"Well, you picked a beautiful place to be buried," Cedar added with his usual cynicism.

"Cedar!" Juniper exclaimed. "That's a horrible thing to say!"

"Guys," Sequoia replied. "It's only water. Believe me, I should know."

The group wandered over to the barrel, still a little leery of its contents. Mesquite sniffed inside the container. "It smells fine. I think he's right. I think it's water," he said and took a little drink himself. "Yep, that's just plain old water."

"Why would a truck be loaded with barrels labeled toxic chemicals inside, when in fact they're just full of water?" Aspen asked.

"Whatever the reason, it has to be bad," Juniper said. "The driver was drugged or something too."

"And that truck was leaking brake fluid the whole way down that road," Cedar added. "I even got some on my fur when it drove over me."

"Something's going on," Mesquite acknowledged. "There's more here than meets the eye."

Just then, the kids heard the sound of movement on the road above. They scampered away from the barrel and into a more hidden area under the sprawling, scraggly arms of a willow bush.

A large black sport utility vehicle, escorted by a police car, pulled up and stopped. The policeman got out of his car and was soon joined by the occupants of the 4x4.

The animals watched as a large man in an olive-drab field jacket, his greasy black hair pulled back into a ponytail, stepped to the edge of road. His right arm was made of metal and a horrible, large three-pronged claw served as his hand. A pair of Soldierjacks, humanistic robot workers built by the Axxes Conglomeration, flanked him on each side. They were scanning the field in front of them, looking for something.

"You sure you guys are missing a barrel?" the deputy asked.

"Take my word for it," Spade grumbled. "You look on the other side of the road. We'll check this side."

The officer moved away and headed across the road. Spade called back to him before he had gotten too far, "If you find it, and it's busted open, then we got a major chemical disaster on our hands. Don't touch it! Call me, first!"

Then, under his breath, but just barely, he murmured one last word to the policeman: "Chump!"

"Did you hear that?" Mesquite exclaimed to the little mammal posse huddled together under the willow.

"Yeah," Cedar snickered, "he called that cop a chump!"

"Not that, you idiot," Mesquite said, frustrated. "That dude with the claw lied and said there's dangerous chemicals in that barrel!"

"So?" Cedar replied.

"So he's the guy behind all this," Aspen interjected. "This guy is as nasty as the day is long."

Spade turned to his mechanical assistants. "Fan out," he ordered. "Find that missing barrel and let's get back to base."

The Soldierjacks plodded down the ravine in separate directions as Spade watched from the road. The heavy, highly advanced machine men made of metal

and computer components were dressed in the typical Axxes worker uniforms — extra tough, black and red uniforms and durable gloves. Helmets with darkly tinted face shields covered their heads.

They both carried standard-issue Flamesaw devices — heavy-duty industrial tools, created exclusively by Axxes, that combined flamethrowers with chainsaws for fast, brutal destruction of forests, buildings or whatever gets in their way.

"They're up to something," Mesquite asserted. "I'm getting in that truck to see what I can find out!"

The uninhibited wolf pup started out abruptly from under the bush toward Spade's vehicle. Before he could get far, Sequoia leaned forward and grabbed him by the tail with his teeth. Mesquite's front paws flew out from under him and his chin hit the ground. He turned and gave Sequoia an angry look.

"What gives?!" Mesquite said with a scowl.

"Hold it," Sequoia said. "Let Juniper g-g-go. She's smaller and f-f-faster."

Aspen backed him up. "Yeah. Juniper should go."

Juniper recoiled at the suggestion. "Me?" she exclaimed. "What if I get caught? I'm the youngest one here! It's Mesquite's idea, let him go."

"C'mon, Juniper," Cedar piped in. "You're always whining

about being the baby — now's your chance to prove yourself."

Juniper looked at him resentfully. "I'm not scared. I'll show you. I'll show all of you!" she said. She wanted desperately to be considered as brave as the others.

The tiny black-footed ferret peered up at the big, black Hummer parked up on the road and crept out of the hedges. She darted for the vehicle and in seconds she was hiding under it and cowering behind the rear wheel.

Spade had wandered off a ways, watching the Soldierjacks probing into the cattails with their Flamesaws. He pulled out a cigar, bit off the end and set it in his mouth. Then he struck a match on his metal arm, lit the stogie and flung the match off into the brush. Amazingly, it didn't start a fire.

Juniper glanced around and saw that the big guy with the metal arm was preoccupied. She stepped out from under the SUV and jumped into it through the door left open by one of the Soldierjacks.

Inside, Juniper dashed around looking for clues. She pounced from one part of the vehicle to the other, not even sure what she was looking for.

Off in the brush, the Soldierjacks were busily searching for the missing barrel. One of them finally happened upon it. The lid was still off, just as Sequoia had left it.

The Soldierjack called out to Spade in a pro-
grammed voice through a transmitter in its helmet.

"Zzt! I found it, sir!" the man-machine shouted. It
held up its arm and waved Spade over.

Spade smiled from the roadside. "Well done, Number
12!" he said and then exhaled a huge plume of ripe cigar
smoke. Spade found it difficult to be complimentary to
any fellow humans, and far easier to be cordial to his
force of Axxes robots.

"We got it!" Spade yelled to the deputy sheriff still
searching the other side of the road. "It spilled out
everywhere!" he continued, lying through his teeth. "I'm
gonna have to call in my Hazmat boys! You better shut
this area down, officer!"

The deputy quickly grabbed his radio and alerted his
dispatch while Spade calmly dialed out on his headset.
Everything was going according to plan.

Meanwhile, Juniper had found and opened Spade's
briefcase in the passenger seat. She started rifling
through it and came across a highly detailed satellite
map of the area they were in. Clearly marked on it was
the scene of the supposed truck accident and a peculiar red "X" up the road a ways and off into the forest,
next to one of the upper branches of the Onahu Creek.

Juniper folded the map as small as she could and

started for the door with it in her mouth. Just then, she saw Spade and the two Soldierjacks, just a few feet away, returning to the Hummer.

She gasped, her eyes wide with horror. She quickly replaced the map and dove under the seat.

Juniper's friends watched helplessly as Spade and the Soldierjacks climbed back into the Hummer and closed the doors. They never saw her get out.

Juniper wheezed when Spade started the engine. She was terrified.

As he shifted the transmission into gear, he noticed the lid to his briefcase was unlatched. He was sure he had fastened it so he checked to make sure the map was still in the briefcase, just in case. Satisfied, he closed it and drove away.

"Oh, great! We'll never be able to catch that truck," Cedar said as Mesquite and Sequoia looked at each other with shock and despair.

"Maybe you guys can't," Aspen said in a rather condescending manner. "But I bet I can."

Aspen took off from the tree limb on which she had been sitting and flew off erratically in the direction the truck was traveling. She really wished she could fly better, but took pride in the fact that she had abilities unique to the team. She considered herself above the others.

"Well, I guess we're walking," Mesquite said to his buddies. They knew it would be awhile until they saw their friend Juniper again. They hoped she wouldn't be discovered and they prayed Aspen could keep up with Spade's vehicle.

Aspen had used up nearly all her energy just to keep pace with Spade's Hummer. It had pulled off the main road and was bouncing down an unused access road, its tires clawing for traction at times to get over rocky edges and loose gravel. She gasped and sputtered and her wings burned with pain. The thin air was really taking its toll. Then she furrowed her brow and redoubled her effort with one last push with all the strength she had left.

"Don't worry, Juniper," she said to herself. "I won't let you down."

Inside the vehicle, Juniper whimpered and trembled in her hiding place under the seat. The large, black boots of a Soldierjack were right in front of her face.

"This is why I don't volunteer for these stupid things," she thought aloud. "That idiot Mesquite should be the one stuck in here!"

Moments later, the Hummer arrived at the secluded Axxes development site. It came to a sudden stop in front of a small construction trailer surrounded by futuristic and ominous equipment on the northwest

bank of a small river. Dozens of Soldierjacks bustled around the site, performing various tasks.

Spade grabbed his briefcase and headed into the trailer while the Soldierjacks with him stepped out and walked stiffly over to a large tracked vehicle that resembled a huge crab made of iron. It had a large, squat circular turret that could hold up to three Soldierjacks and jutting outward from its front were two long metal arms. One had a giant hydraulic pincer at the end and its twin featured an immense circular saw blade. The 25-ton Crabtank is one of many custom-designed Axxes pieces of machinery, which look more at home on a military base than in a national park grabbing and cutting down trees. It was extremely efficient at deforestation.

Axxes had two dozen of the armored monsters as well as nearly 400 Soldierjacks spread out across the national park, razing the highland wilderness of its dead pine trees at an unprecedented pace. It was because of his ingenious inventions that he landed the contract to cut down the dead wood in the first place. The Rockies were a tinderbox just waiting to burn.

Juniper sighed with relief and peered out from her hiding place inside Spade's 4x4. She jumped up on the backseat and peeked out the window at her surroundings,

looking aghast at what was going on around her.

Juniper soon realized that the doors were locked. She was trapped inside. "I just can't win!" she exclaimed.

Looking around, she noticed that the front window was open just a crack. Spade loved his cigars, but he didn't like his new Hummer to reek of foul tobacco smoke.

The little female ferret jumped up onto the armrest of the driver's door and stretched upward until her little paws reached the top of the window. Squirming and squiggling her way through the crack, she finally dropped to the ground outside her vehicular prison with a soft thump.

Spade's huge boot prints, and the scent trail from his cigar, easily gave away his position. "I'm going to get that map and let everyone know about this place," she whispered to herself.

Juniper skittered over to the aluminum shelter Spade had entered. She worked her way over to a window, ducking all the while from Soldierjacks going about their business.

Juniper shimmied up a pine tree next to the building and then down a limb until she was perfectly positioned next to the window. Peering inside, she could see and hear everything going on inside.

The pony-tailed man with the metal arm had his big, dirty boots up on the desk and his back to the window. His smelly cigar stub was crushed out in an old tuna can that was serving as an ashtray. Over his broad shoulders, she could see the briefcase sitting open on the desk and the map lying right on top. He was leaning rearward in his chair as he reached out with his left hand, opened a drawer, and pulled out a sandwich wrapped in plastic.

After unwrapping it and taking an ample bite, he punched a few buttons on the keyboard perched below a high-tech monitor. Then he sloppily licked a big glob of mayonnaise off his thumb. In a couple of seconds, the videophone came to life, showing the sinister face of an older silver-haired man.

"Mr. Axxes," the one-armed man, just a few feet behind the glass in front of Juniper, said with a certain amount of swagger. "It's Burt Spade, sir."

"I can see who it is, you dimwit," Nathan Axxes replied, aggravated. "Now report."

"Well, we have everything ready," Burt stammered. "The cops shut down the Grand Lake entrance just like you said they would once I told them the barrel was full of chemicals, not water. Our own Hazmat team of Soldierjacks is on their way and under orders to treat

the spill like it's dangerous and take their sweet time cleaning it up."

Axxes broke in. "Miranda has already influenced the authorities out there to keep the park closed, using road repair as a cover-up so the public doesn't get spooked. That gives you and your team less than 48 hours to bring in the Hazmat vehicle convoy and have the rigs with the biotech weapons equipment hidden onboard slip away and get to your location where you are now. You should have complete freedom to do what you need while the local constables unwittingly provide security for the whole operation."

"You sure are a genius, Mr. Axxes," Spade said in a tone that was part authentic compliment and part sugarcoated flattery.

Nathan saw through Spade's comment and jabbed back, "If only my loyal followers were half so, Mr. Spade...."

"Hey, boss, how come we didn't just spill the real chemicals?" Spade asked. "We got thousands of gallons of pesticide up here. Who cares about this place anyway?"

"Because, my handicapped heathen," Axxes answered, "not only are those chemicals extremely expensive, but if we had dumped thirteen barrels all

over the place like your under-talented truck driver was supposed to do, then the insecticide would corrupt the mind-control virus you're going to actually be pumping into the creek upstream. It kills more than just pine beetles, my friend."

Juniper couldn't believe what she was hearing. She scooted closer to the window to make sure she didn't miss a thing.

"How is the spring runoff looking?" Axxes asked, referring to the melting of the massive amounts of mountain snow that had piled up over the winter months.

"Fantastic," Spade replied. "It was a good year for snowfall. The rivers are running high."

A wicked smile crept across Nathan's face. "Perfect. Once you are sure the digital virus is draining into the creek from there at ground zero, it should take less than an hour to flow into the Colorado River and from there, it will spread and infect all those states siphoning off that water from Kansas to southern California."

"Impressive," Spade said, once again blown away by the grandeur of his employer's evil schemes.

"Oh, it's more than that," Axxes boasted. "I am confident that the biotech plague we're about to unleash will maintain its integrity once absorbed in the crops

that are irrigated by the tainted water."

Spade didn't quite comprehend Nathan's last comment. His confused look translated across the videophone, so Axxes dumbed it down for him. "In other words, you moron, when they water a field of apples and some idiot in Chicago eats it, he will also be mine to control. The potential is global!"

"That's incredible, boss!" Spade said excitedly. "But I still don't understand how you actually gain control of them."

"I worked with Doctor Kaustik for months on this," Axxes explained. "He's the true brilliance behind the biotech. His ingenious transmission method involves first getting the virus to embed in the brain. Since the pathogen is actually liquidized data, it can't even be detected.

"Then we hack into phone transmissions and send the control code. It instantly downloads and installs once the brain has been infected. Look how easy it was to manipulate your little truck driver."

"Speaking of which, what do you want me to do with the truck, Mr. Axxes?" Burt inquired.

"Tow it away," Nathan said. "Make sure the authorities don't get to it. They might just figure out the brake lines were cut and the containers weren't secured."

"And what about the driver? They took him to a hospital already," Spade added.

As Axxes spoke, he leaned forward, closer to the video screen on his side of the teleconference, and squinted his eyes. He was trying to make out something behind Spade. "I don't really care about him. Let him stay in a coma for all I care...."

Axxes abruptly stopped talking. "Spade, is that a scrawny raccoon peeking in the window behind you?"

Spade spun around in his chair, nearly falling off. He caught a glimpse of Juniper's face pressed up against the glass.

Jumping to his feet, he threw his sandwich down on the map and quickly closed his briefcase. Then he bolted to the door, threw it open and looked to the side of the trailer at the window.

She was gone.

Spade looked around, eventually walking the entire perimeter of the trailer but didn't see anything. He came back inside after about a minute to finish his report with his overseer in Los Angeles.

"Whatever it was, it's gone now," Spade told him.

Axxes was getting antsy. He didn't trust anything or anyone. "Just don't screw this up, Spade. No witnesses, no mercy. Use whatever means are at your disposal

to ensure my plans are properly executed. Apply extreme force if you must. I won't tolerate failure, Mr. Spade."

"Understood, sir," Burt tried to appease him. "Extreme force is what I'm best at."

From her hiding place on the roof of Spade's trailer, Juniper was trying to decide what to do next. She was fully aware of the awful plans about to take place. By herself, the little girl ferret knew she couldn't stop them. She needed her friends.

"Juniper!" She was startled when she suddenly heard her name. She looked up in the tree beside the trailer to see who was calling her.

"Aspen!" she shouted upon seeing her peregrine falcon friend perched on the evergreen. "I'm so glad you're here! How did you find me?"

"I followed the 4x4 all the way here," Aspen replied. "And a black-footed ferret scurrying around on the roof of a trailer is pretty hard to miss from the sky."

"Where are the boys? Are they here too?" Juniper inquired.

"Are you kidding?" Aspen chortled. "Those grounders can't keep up with me. They're probably a couple miles back yet."

Juniper scampered quietly over to the edge of the trailer roof and jumped onto an outstretched branch

next to Aspen. Dozens of Soldierjacks were keeping busy with their chores all around them. Most of them were focused on clearing an area on the bank of the creek while others were setting up camouflage nets and installing some kind of perimeter defenses. The Crabtank fired up its engine and maneuvered down the trailhead, crunching sticks and gravel alike under its hefty rotating tracks.

"Aspen! I know everything!" Juniper blurted. "We gotta get the team together and shut them down!"

"Just a minute," Aspen said. Her wings and her lungs were still recovering from her pursuit. "Tell me what you know."

As Juniper relayed everything she saw and heard while spying through the window, Burt Spade came out of the trailer and walked over to his Hummer.

He opened the tailgate and popped the latches to what looked like an enormous gun case. Next, he reached over with his left arm and, after clicking a sequence of buttons and switches, disconnected his artificial arm with the three-pronged claw. He set it inside the huge storage caddy, pushing it firmly down into the slot perfectly cut for it into a giant block of foam.

Then he pulled out another interchangeable arm and snapped it into place. This one looked like a high-powered

cannon. It had an array of buttons on one side, ovular exhaust ports on top and even a slot for Spade's left arm to hold it since it was so heavy. He slapped a magazine into it and trudged over to the riverside where his robot crew was busy working.

Spade issued some orders to a pair of Soldierjacks and they brought over a set of ten-foot-long iron beams to where Spade was standing. He had them put the girders in place across of pair of deeply buried, fairly flat boulders that jutted out into the rushing river.

Burt set the barrel of his cannon-arm against the flat bottom end of the beam and fired. A steel spike shot through the one-inch-thick metal and buried itself into the rock it was sitting on. A piston inside the giant nail gun loaded the next eight-inch spike into place and Spade continued pinning the beams into place. He was building a level platform for the biotech equipment to rest on which was due to arrive anytime.

Spade's nail gun arm was one of his favorites. Not only could it hold and shoot a variety of fasteners from rivets to bolts, but it also was extremely intimidating. With it attached to his torso, Spade was indeed a living weapon.

Still monitoring the whole operation from the safety

of the tree, Juniper proposed a plan to Aspen. "We wait for the boys to get here and then we sneak into this here trailer. The one-armed man's briefcase holds a map to this place we're at and I'll bet all kinds of documents about what they're up to. We smuggle the briefcase out and then drop it off at the nearest ranger station. Those guys will freak when they see what these lowlifes are up to!"

Aspen thought about it for a few seconds. "Not bad, little girl," Aspen said. "Alright, I'll fly back, find the boys and guide them back here. I'll let them know what's going on and what you want to do. I think it's a good idea. You were very brave.

"Meanwhile, you stay put. Just keep an eye on these guys and stay out of sight. I'll be back with the others in a jiffy. Deal?"

Juniper smiled. "Deal!"

Aspen hopped off her branch and glided down toward the trail that led into the hidden site. In a few moments, she was soaring south and on her way to find Mesquite, Sequoia and Cedar.

Back in the tree, Juniper watched the activity of Spade and his Soldierjacks as they continued preparing their secret base. She felt good about herself and proud of what she did. Minutes ticked by as she sat

there, 15 feet off the ground, observing the enemy. A ferret's place is not in a tree, she thought to herself.

She decided to push her luck.

Juniper worked her way down from the lodgepole pine and crept over to the trailer door. She figured she could break into the trailer herself, push the briefcase off the desk and then slide it out the door and into the woods. She was smart enough to know that she could not lift it. She was just too small.

Spade had closed the door tight and without rotating the door handle that was beyond her reach by nearly two feet, she knew she couldn't open it.

Thinking that perhaps the window she had looked through earlier might be ajar, she ran over to it next but could plainly see it was still closed as well. If she wanted to get in this trailer, it would have to be through the front door.

Looking around, Juniper noticed a shovel lying on the ground. An idea was formulating in her head.

She pushed on the shovel. It was harder than she first thought, but she finally steered it into position with the wooden handle resting at the base of the door.

Then she hoisted the handle over her head and slowly started walking backwards toward the end with the metal trowel. It was incredibly heavy. Her muscles were

shaking under the strain, but with each step, the handle rose ever higher until finally she was able to set it on the door handle. The weight of the shovel alone almost popped it open, but not quite.

Juniper stepped out from under the shovel that angled up to the door's handgrip and paused to look around while trying to catch her breath. The coast was clear.

With renewed energy, the female ferret ran up the shovel and jumped on the door handle. It turned just enough to release the latch and it swung open. Juniper, and the shovel, fell to the ground with a bit more noise than she had estimated. She stood motionless, on the doorstep to Spade's trailer, listening for the sound of approaching footsteps.

After a few moments, she realized she hadn't been detected so she pushed the shovel out of the entryway and made her way over to the desk.

She hopped first up on Spade's chair and then onto the desk in one quick, decisive movement. There sat the briefcase. Juniper was elated.

*****

The boys had grown tired from walking, but they

pressed on, knowing their friend could be in trouble.

"I'm tired," Cedar bellowed. "Let's stop for a minute." Being a badger, he naturally had the shortest legs.

"Yeah. My feet hurt," Sequoia chimed in.

"No!" Mesquite shot back. "We have to keep going! Juniper needs us."

"She shouldn't have gotten caught in the first place!" Cedar said.

"It was your bright idea to send her up to that truck, if you recall, Cedar," Mesquite said shrewdly. "I should have gone. I wouldn't have got caught!"

"Yeah, right," Cedar replied. "You definitely would've got caught."

"No I wouldn't! You take that back!" the wolf pup said, and he bristled the hair on his back to make himself seem bigger.

Cedar wasn't intimidated. "Make me, puppy-breath!"

Mesquite jumped at Cedar and they started to wrestle. Somehow they found enough strength to get into a fight. They snarled and snipped at each other with their immature animal voices. Sequoia sat down, rolled his eyes and sighed.

"Excuse me!" a voice suddenly screeched from above. It startled all three of them. "When you two are done screwing around, I have something to tell you!"

The tussling twosome froze in place.

"Aspen!" Sequoia blurted out as he looked up at her, squinting from the sun. "What is it? D-d-did you find Juniper? Is she alright?"

"She's up ahead a ways, at an Axxes-controlled secret construction site," Aspen said. "She did good. She found out they're going to pump some mind-control stuff in the river. We gotta stop them!"

Mesquite kicked Cedar off him. "Show us the way!"

CHAPTER 7

Back at Spade's trailer, Juniper had to clear a path off the desk so she could more easily shove the briefcase to the floor.

She stepped toward the tuna can ashtray to move it out of the way. The smell of rancid fish oil combined with old, smoky cigars triggered Juniper's gag reflex. She almost retched. Wincing, she plugged her nose with one hand and used her foot to scoot the source of her dismay as far away as possible.

All of a sudden, a loud voice boomed from just outside the trailer. It scared Juniper so bad she almost fell off the desk.

It was Spade. He was back. "Hey!" he screamed at the top of his lungs. "Which one of you nimrods left a shovel lying in front of my trailer?"

Juniper's eyes were wide with fright as she heard his heavy footsteps right outside. Terrified, she ran across the desk and leaped into the wastebasket, burying herself under yesterday's newspaper.

"And which one of you left my trailer door open?" he hollered. He was livid. Soldierjacks were usually very

mindful and well disciplined. Spade stepped inside his trailer and looked around. Everything seemed in order. Furious, he stood in the entryway of the trailer and called to the nearest Soldierjack who had just finished setting up some camouflage rigging.

"Hey, you!" the burly bully screamed. "Did you do this?"

The robot turned to face his human master. "Zzt! Negative, sir."

There was no answer besides admitting guilt that would have made Spade happy. "You calling me a liar, boy?"

In its monotone, digitized voice, the Soldierjack replied again, "Negative, sir."

Spade's temper got the best of him. He raised his weaponized arm at the worker drone and fired. A thunderclap filled the air as the metal spike tore through the unwary Soldierjack's chest and embedded into a tree trunk behind it. The drone fell to its knees and then flat on its faceplate with an apple-sized, smoking hole in its midsection.

"Let that be a lesson to all of you!" Burt exclaimed loud enough for all his Soldierjacks to hear. "Don't mess with my stuff!"

Buried in the trashcan, Juniper cowered, shivering. The blast from Spade's nail gun accessory echoed throughout the trailer and shook the thin-walled compartment

to its core. She heard his big boots come back inside the tiny trailer and he slammed the door shut behind him. He sat down hard in his chair and shuffled papers around on his desk.

Spade had come back looking for the installation schematics for the generator that powered the biotech lab. He found them half buried underneath his briefcase, which he picked up and set on the floor next to him. Then he spent some long minutes reviewing the diagrams and writing notes while Juniper, still covered up in the wastebasket just inches away, tried to stay quiet.

She was stuck. She wondered how much longer it would be until her friends arrived.

After a while, the sound of vehicles approaching got Spade to stand up and look out the window. It was the first of the laboratory equipment trucks disguised as Hazmat vehicles. Two Soldierjacks were inside, wearing chemical suits to emphasize their deceitful purpose.

"About time," Spade grumbled. Then he turned and left the trailer, making sure to close the door behind. He escorted the falsified Hazmat vehicle down to the river and supervised the unloading of it.

After a few seconds, Juniper peered out from the rim of the trashcan. "That was a close one," she said

aloud. "I gotta get out of here!"

She hopped free and clear of her hiding place and moved around the chair on her way to the door. That's when she noticed the briefcase sitting right in front of her. A grin came across her catlike face but soon disappeared when she realized the door handle was once again out of reach and, worse, the door only opened inward.

Outside, Aspen landed in the same tree she had left Juniper sitting in when she flew off to bring the boys. "Juniper!" she shouted as quietly as she could. "Juniper! Where are you?"

"Well?" Mesquite asked Aspen from his concealed spot underneath Spade's Hummer along with Cedar and Sequoia. "Where is she? You said she'd be here!"

Sneaking into the site's perimeter had not been easy. Soldierjacks were patrolling all along the outskirts of the location and sensors were being set up every 50 yards. Axxes sure didn't want anyone even getting close to their hideout.

Aspen was starting to get mad. "Juniper! Answer me!"

"I hate to even s-s-say this, guys," Sequoia said, "but I w-w-wonder if that shot we heard as we were s-s-sneaking in here was for her."

"Don't think like that!" Mesquite scolded him.

"It can't be so," Cedar assured them. "One of their robots laying over there has a fresh hole in it. That sucker was the victim of the shot we heard, not Juniper. I'm betting the sound of it scared her off and she's half a mile from here."

Aspen called out one last time. "Juniper!"

Then Aspen heard a tapping sound on the window of the trailer. She looked down and saw Juniper balancing on the back of a chair and rapping on the glass with her little ferret paws.

"Aspen! You made it!" her little voice called out from inside. "I'm in here! Open the door!"

The young falcon left the tree and landed softly on the shovel still in the dirt in front of the door. She turned back to her teammates to fill them in: "Well, I found her. She didn't listen to me and she left the tree and then got stuck inside the trailer. Trying to be a hero, I guess. Let's get this door open."

The boys stepped out from under the vehicle and gathered next to Aspen.

"Sequoia, it's all yours, big guy," Mesquite said.

The bear cub rumbled up to the door, stood up on his hind legs and used his front paws to pull down on the door handle. The door swung open and Juniper ran out.

"We w-w-were worried about you!" Sequoia said.

"Next time listen to me!" Aspen shrieked, upset but relieved at the same time.

"I'm sorry," she said. "I should have listened."

"What you did was pretty dumb, Juniper," Mesquite said. "We didn't know what happened to you or..."

Cedar interrupted the emotional oration with some degree of urgency; "Hey! Let's talk about all this once we got the briefcase and are safely away from here!"

"Oh yeah!" Juniper said, "How could I forget? It's right in here." She went back inside and motioned for the rest to follow.

They plodded in and saw it right away.

"See? I told you!" Juniper said, standing proudly next to it. "This should ruin their day once the rangers get hold of it!"

"What is th-th-that awful smell?" Sequoia grimaced.

Juniper realized he had picked up the scent of Spade's ashtray. "You really don't want to know. Trust me."

Mesquite walked up to the attaché case and grabbed the handle with his teeth. Even with his head held high, he wasn't tall enough to lift it clear of the floor.

Sequoia saw Mesquite struggling and offered to help. "Do you w-w-want me to carry that thing?" he asked.

Mesquite shook his head. With the handle still in his mouth, he tried to answer as best he could. "Don't

worry. I got this," he said, mumbling. Then he proved he was able by turning around and easily dragging the case behind him. It slid quite smoothly.

Cedar led the way as the five critters strode out of the trailer and darted under Spade's 4x4 again.

"Okay," Cedar said. "Same way out as we got in. Aspen, take to the trees and watch for the bad guys. Oh, and Juniper, stay close and pay attention!"

Aspen hopped and launched herself into the air and soon touched down on the next tree over. She looked around for a little while and then waved her wing for the rest to follow.

The forest animal foursome, one with a briefcase in its mouth, ran single file from under the Hummer and to a clump of trees 20 feet away. Then they made another dash for it, this time behind a large, moss-covered rock, and soon they had gotten pretty far.

Large, empty Axxes equipment containers were scattered about the area and offered great cover from the ever-watchful eyes of the Soldierjack sentries.

Aspen was finding it challenging in her role as lookout. The place was swarming with robots and all sorts of obstacles, natural or not, provided concealment of the movement of the bad guys as much as it did for the heroes.

After another successful rush, they realized they were about to break out of the perimeter. Just over one last hill scattered with scrub oak and they were home free.

Without warning, three loud blasts discharged in the air from back behind them and echoed out, bouncing off the mountains. Then they heard the screaming.

It was Spade. He had returned to his Hummer to switch arms again and found his trailer door left open. He immediately saw that his briefcase was missing. Discovering animal tracks and long drag marks leading away from his portable office in the woods, he went berserk. Enraged, he fired three spikes into the sky.

"Animals have stolen my briefcase!" he roared to his Soldierjacks. "Spread out! Find them! Find my brief-case. Now!"

A column of Soldierjacks suddenly appeared, march-ing in a line directly to the front of them. They were conducting a sweep of the terrain, searching for the animal thieves. "Zzt! Intruder alert! Intruder alert!"

"Oh no!" Cedar yelped. "Back up! Back up!"

The animals scrambled in the other direction, slipping and tripping as they ran and losing precious ground doing so.

Flushed by the oncoming Soldierjacks, the animal

friends soon found themselves almost all the way back in the center of Spade's camp. Mesquite looked down and noticed the attaché he had been tugging along this whole time had left an obvious plowed trail, leading right to where they were.

Soldierjacks were pouring into the center of camp with their Flamesaws at the ready. With his chest heaving and his face red and sweaty, Spade lumbered along, following the drag marks. His huge cannon-arm was at the ready.

"Those animals must be after my sandwich!" he grumbled aloud, furious that he had put it in his briefcase earlier when Axxes called. "I'm going to nail them to the ground for this!"

"Guys! Get out of there!" Aspen screamed from the treetops. "There's too many of them!" She swooped down to join her friends. Better to be together than apart, she thought. Besides, she was an easy target in the branches above.

"We gotta hide!" Juniper pleaded, panting.

"They'll b-b-be on us any minute," Sequoia said as he stepped slowly backwards.

"They won't stop until they find that briefcase!" Cedar declared.

Mesquite spit the handle out of his mouth and the

carryall fell to the ground in front of him with a thump. "Then I say we give it to them!"

Trudging through the underbrush, the circle of Soldierjacks around the site slowly closed like the tightening coils of a constrictor. Spade, meanwhile, was closing in on his quarry with every step, with an obvious trail that would lead him right to the bandits and his prized possession. He had several valuable documents and digital files related to their covert operation inside that case. He knew Axxes would be furious if he found it was stolen or lost.

Stepping past some discarded stove-sized metal containers that once held the camouflage netting now cloaking his site from prying eyes, Spade continued to follow the briefcase's rut. It led around the base of a large aspen tree where, finally, he found it.

There it sat, in the shade of the tree, leaning up against the trunk as if put there by gentle hands. Completely intact and still latched shut, it was none the worse for wear except for some tiny teeth marks on the handle and some dirt and scrape marks on its base.

"Ha!" Spade bellowed. He was relieved. He reached down, picked it up and scanned the area for the furry burglars. They had to be close.

In a few seconds, the Soldierjack guards closed in

and stood shoulder to shoulder in a giant circumference, surrounding their leader.

"Nothing?" Spade asked the nearest drone.

"Zzt! Nothing, sir," it relayed. "This area is clear and secure."

"Amazing," Spade said, just glad to have his briefcase back. He paused for a while, looking all around and listening for any clues as to the whereabouts of the mischievous mammals that apparently tried to steal his lunch. He wanted to deal them some punishment.

Seeing nothing, Spade turned and headed back for his 4x4. After just a few steps, he glimpsed some animal tracks and bent grasses that led into one of the empty metal camouflage containers set off to the side. He halted, smiled, and decided to use a little discretion. Spade considered himself a rather shrewd and clever man - a true disciple of Nathan Axxes.

"Alright, Soldierjacks, listen up!" he shouted back to his force, barely able to hide his true intentions. "Get back to work! And get this area cleaned up! Load these camo-boxes on the truck and get them out of here!"

Then he motioned for one of the Soldierjacks to come closer. He put his real arm around it and, with a depraved grin, whispered his final orders so only it could hear him. "Take these containers to the top of

the continental divide," he said scornfully, "and throw
them off the steepest cliff you can find."

CHAPTER 8

The Natural Forces felt the black metal box they were hiding in suddenly jostle about and then rise off the ground. A pair of Soldierjacks had grabbed each end and was carrying it over to a truck that was parked not far away.

"Where do you think they're taking us?" Aspen asked the others. It was pitch black inside the container.

"Hopefully, back to town someplace," Cedar said.

"Or maybe to the dump!" Sequoia said excitedly. He had eaten many meals by digging around landfills. Sequoia seemed to always be hungry.

"I can't believe we got away," Juniper added. "I thought we were goners for sure."

"Good leaders have good ideas," Mesquite smugly said. If it weren't so dark, his four friends would have seen that he was holding his chin up high with a prudish manner.

"Here we go again..." Cedar griped, weary of his wolf pup pal's constant self-promotion.

"Oh, really?" Aspen interjected. "If you had just let Sequoia take the briefcase, then the drag marks you left

behind wouldn't have put us in danger in the first place!"

"You don't know that!" Mesquite snipped. "He's not much bigger than me!"

"Am too," the bear cub said.

"Are not," Mesquite fired back. "And besides, Juniper's the one who started all this in the first place. This whole thing was her idea."

"Hey!" Juniper exclaimed. "Don't make me your escape goat!"

There was an awkward moment of silence and Juniper heard one of the critters start to chuckle.

"What did you just say?" Mesquite asked.

"You heard me," Juniper said, not wanting to repeat her last statement.

"Did you just say..." Mesquite retorted but was interrupted by Sequoia.

"You m-m-mean scapegoat, Juniper," the little bear said as he fought back from giggling. "You meant to s-s-say 'don't make me your scapegoat.'"

Juniper was embarrassed and frustrated. "Whatever!" she fumed.

"Shh!" Cedar scolded loudly. "Pay attention!"

The box they were riding in courtesy of the robots that were carrying it suddenly stopped moving. Then it rose up, was set back down onto something hard and then pushed

a few feet into place. Their metal container bumped up against another metallic object with a solid thud.

"I think they put us in the back of a truck," Cedar said.

"Yeah, I agree," Aspen said.

They could barely make out that the Soldierjacks were walking away. After a long pause, they heard them return and then a repeat of the same sounds as before and another metal box bumped up against theirs.

Then came the distinct sound of the truck's tailgate slamming shut and the animals knew they were in the bed of a pickup and about to be taken away.

"I gotta give you props, Mesquite, for coming up with the idea of ditching the briefcase and hiding in this box," Cedar said. "Most of your ideas are pretty stupid, but with this one you got lucky."

"Thanks," Mesquite replied. "I think."

Aspen wasn't so sure. "Don't start celebrating until we're safely out of here, guys. Something doesn't feel right. This whole escape is just going too well."

Mesquite didn't want to hear any of it. "Quit being so worried, everyone," he tried to assure them. "I'm positive we'll be dropped off soon enough."

The truck's doors opened and then closed in unison as the Soldierjacks entered the cab. Then the engine turned over and the transmission shifted into gear.

Soon the truck was jouncing and bouncing over the bumpy landscape as it made its way slowly out of Spade's construction site in the high woods.

The kids were having a hard time staying on their feet inside their secret hiding place in the back of the truck. They were also experiencing ever-happier feelings with every yard they were being driven further away from Spade and his horde of androids.

After nearly half an hour of jittery travel, the truck's ride suddenly smoothed out. They were on asphalt again.

"Isn't it amazing?" Juniper said.

"What?" Mesquite replied. "That my plans usually turn out perfectly?"

"No, you idiot," Juniper continued. "That robots can drive trucks."

"I don't c-c-care what they can do," Sequoia said. "As long as they t-t-take me somewhere where there's food."

"Geez, Sequoia," Cedar quipped, "didn't you just eat half the sandwich in that briefcase?"

"Well, yeah, but it wasn't enough," Sequoia replied. "And besides, it had too much mayonnaise on it."

Back at Spade's hideout, work was progressing again, without interruption, on setting up the bio-lab. Another counterfeit Hazmat vehicle had arrived and

was being put into place. This truck, a triple-axle heavy-duty water tanker, would serve as the primary holding tank for the infected water. It had been reconfigured to draw up to 4,000 gallons of the clean river water into its holding tank where it would then become saturated with the liquefied digital virus. When the mind-control strain stabilized into the water molecules, it would then be released back downstream.

Once implemented, the whole process would take less than an hour per tankful. Running 24 hours a day, at peak capacity, the depraved secret operation could push 96,000 gallons of contaminated water onto an unsuspecting public each and every day. Axxes estimated the tainted water would reach the Hoover Dam in about 200 hours and then another day to flow down the Mulholland Aqueduct and into the city of Los Angeles – the primary target for his plan.

All Spade still had left to install was the power generator, the computer array that produced an endless supply of the mind-control virus, and the system that turned the digital code into a dissolvable, fluid form. Two more truckloads and Spade was in business.

Meanwhile, inside the metal camo-box, the fivesome grew anxious as they waited for the truck to stop. They could tell that they were traversing through a

series of switchbacks and gaining in elevation as the truck headed ever east. The truck was steadily moving away from the town of Grand Lake and up toward Trail Ridge Road, which is the highest continuous highway in the United States.

"Where are these guys going?" Juniper said, breaking the silence. It awoke Cedar and Mesquite who had dozed off in the darkness of their temporary sanctuary.

"We there yet?" Cedar groggily asked.

"It's getting colder in here," Aspen added. "We are definitely going up." Being a falcon, she, of all the animals, was very familiar with changes in elevation.

The truck suddenly slowed to a near stop and then abruptly turned off the paved road and onto an irregular trail. The boxes bumped and banged against each other until finally the whole vehicle stopped.

The animals heard the doors open and shut and the sound of the robot's footsteps crunching on the ground outside. When the tailgate was pulled open, the whole truck shuddered as they let it fall. Next, the metal container loaded in last was pulled out of the truck and then for a while there was nothing but silence.

Soon, the Soldierjacks returned and hoisted out the box with the animals hidden inside.

"Finally!" Mesquite said excitedly. "Home free, boys and girls!"

"Well, don't pop the top until we know the coast is clear, you moron," Cedar warned.

The Soldierjacks once again maneuvered themselves and the second container they were carrying to the edge of a cliff that plummeted over a half mile to the bottom. The empty metal box they had thrown over the side several seconds before had finally just stopped bashing and smashing itself against the jutting rocks that covered the cliff walls. That container had been flattened and torn to shreds during its horrible descent. They were at 13,000 feet in elevation, above treeline. The wind was whipping all around. Off in the distance, a hawk cried out.

Aspen grew agitated. She fluttered about and spread her wings. "Something's wrong!" She shouted. "We gotta get out!"

Following orders, the Soldierjacks mindlessly and flawlessly carried out their assignment. With their arms swinging like pendulums in perfect unison, they tossed the aluminum container with the five young animal stowaways inside into the thin mountain air and off the side of the cliff.

Miranda Wright flew into Denver on one of the Axxes corporation's private jets. Nathan owns a small personal fleet of luxury aircraft that permits him, and his staff, freedom of movement across the globe with virtually no detection and no obstacles. The flight from Los Angeles was smooth and uneventful.

She brought two of her personal assistants along. One of them was driving the limousine she had waiting for them at the executive airport terminal.

During the nearly three-hour drive to Grand Lake along Interstate-70, Miranda used her phone to continue in support of the field operation by manipulation, domination and deceit. She was always able to cover up her company's tactical movements by spinning actual happenings and disclaiming eyewitness accounts.

As the primary spokesperson and legal authority for Axxes, Miranda excelled at her job. She loved to deceive others and her fondness for exploiting weakness in those around her made, and kept, Nathan incredibly wealthy.

From the back of the rented luxury automobile, Miranda was busy convincing a reporter who wanted to do a story on the closing of the park to instead pursue a scoop she had planted about a double homicide in the next county over, while at the same time finishing a press release on her laptop about the fabricated success her company was having in eliminating the pine beetle infestation.

With Ms. Wright on their side, Axxes and Spade were moving at a breakneck pace to initiate their wicked plot.

Her other line rang. It was Nathan. She cut short her conversation with the bewildered reporter and clicked over to speak with her boss.

"Hello, Nathan," she said in a calm and sultry tone.

"Good evening, Miranda," Axxes replied from his California office. "I trust all is well and the game is still in play."

"Oh, most certainly," she said. "I am on my way to the site now. You are right about the people out here; they are so unsophisticated, so gullible."

Nathan snickered. "For you, my dear, it should be like wielding puppets."

"How long do you need me to stay here, Nathan?" she asked. Her car was headed up into the foothills as the sun began its slow descent behind the mountains.

"Just a few days," he assured her. "Once the equipment is up and running, it could practically go on forever. We'll pull out before winter comes. We should have spread quite an epidemic by then."

"I can't believe the military turned us away," she added and then sent her press release to five dozen media outlets with the touch of a button. "You would have thought an idea like this would have been of significant interest to them."

"I surmise even they were scared of something this powerful," Nathan said with a sneer.

She liked his answer. "True," she said, "but I also believe that they didn't think it could be done. No doubt they underestimated you, sir."

"That they did, my dear," Axxes hissed. "That they did."

*****

As soon as the box was thrown off the mountainside and the Soldierjacks had just turned around, an immense explosion of turquoise light burst out from it. As the lid flew open, five animals once trapped inside instantly enlarged and thrust free of its deadly fall.

With her majestic wings spread wide, Aspen soared clear and swooped around, ready to catch any of her

friends who couldn't reach the cliff walls.

Plummeting downward, the four transformed super animals angled themselves and stretched to grasp the side of the mountain.

Sequoia, with the longest reach, made contact first. His giant hand clinched to an outcropping of jagged stone like an anchor while his body scraped and slammed against the mountainside. He was sore, but safe and clinging for his life.

Far below the giant grizzly, Cedar finally managed to sink his claws into a craggy ledge and stop his fall. A horrible 30-foot scar carved into the cliff from all ten of his knife-like nails told the tale of his own fortunate rescue.

Mesquite and Juniper weren't so lucky. The transformed man-wolf realized he couldn't reach the mountain even with the mystical spear staff that appeared in his hand whenever he morphed and saw his ferret friend, just a few feet away, was in the same predicament.

Thinking fast, he barked out his plan while they plunged into the rocky abyss: "Juniper! Grab my spear and I'll throw you to the mountainside!"

Mesquite thrust his lance for her to grab and once she did, he swung it in a powerful arc that propelled Juniper, tumbling through the air, toward the mountain.

She scratched and clawed at the uneven rocks until finally managing to stop herself, 50 feet below Cedar.

Cascading ever downward, gravity pulling on him with full force, Mesquite knew Aspen would save him. With his spear held outward in both hands, he watched as she streaked down and grabbed hold with her powerful talons. Like a parachute deploying, his freefall jolted to a sudden stop and the super-powered falcon warrior-woman flew him back up to the top of the mountain.

He turned to look down and saw the container they had just been in smash against the rocks below. It flattened as it collapsed in on itself into a twisted shard of giant shrapnel and then recoiled back into the air, somersaulting and spinning as it did.

Looking back up he was glad to have a member of the team with the power of flight. "Thanks, Aspen," he said, exhaling loudly. "Perfect timing."

She looked down at him and smiled. "Hey, nice job saving Juniper back there. I don't think I could have got you both."

Like a bizarre zoological hang glider, Aspen flew Mesquite past the rest of the team who were climbing upward to the mountaintop. Sequoia had already breeched the edge and was pulling himself over just as Aspen set down her precious cargo back on solid ground.

"That was a close one!" Sequoia said as he caught his breath.

"Too close," Mesquite answered.

They peered over the steep edge to watch Juniper use her super speed to bound past Cedar and crest the drop-off on her own.

Sequoia got on his knees and reached his powerful arm over the edge as Cedar neared the top. The badger reached out and grasped the grizzly's giant mitt and was promptly lifted like a rag doll out of harm's way.

"Thanks, big guy," Cedar said with his teeth still clenched. He was furious. Somebody was going to pay dearly for throwing them off a mountain.

His chest heaving, Cedar turned to find the ones responsible and vent his anger, but the summit was empty. The Soldierjacks missed the entire spectacle and were driving away down the road nearly a mile away.

From their viewpoint at 13,000 feet, the national park was a magnificent site. The sun was sinking low in the sky and the evening clouds moved in, filtering its rays, and cast an orange-purple hue over the expansive vistas all around them. Snow-capped peaks absorbed the sunset's colors and long shadows blanketed the valleys below.

The mammals stood there in silence, taking in the

majesty of nature at its finest and realizing how lucky they were to be alive.

Mesquite finally spoke. "It will be dark soon. Tomorrow, we shut them down. At daylight, we alert the authorities and bring the fight to them."

"Alert the authorities how?" Aspen asked. "We gave up the briefcase."

Mesquite smiled. "We did, but before putting it where the one-armed man could find it, Sequoia and I opened it and took out everything we could. Then we filled it with branches and closed it back up. He probably still doesn't know we got all his dirty little secrets."

"You sneaky devils," Aspen commended.

"Only one problem," Mesquite said. "We stashed the documents and CDs we stole in that box we were hiding in that's now at the bottom of the mountain. Hopefully, they survived the fall.

"So here's the plan," Mesquite continued. "We split up. Aspen, take Cedar and find that box before it gets too dark. Rip it open and, at daybreak, take the evidence to the nearest ranger station. Sequoia, Juniper and I will head back to the site and watch it from a safe distance until you two come and find us tomorrow. We'll only intervene if it looks like they're ready to launch their virus."

"Let's do this!" Cedar snarled, then ran to the edge of the cliff and leaped off.

Aspen followed his crazy stunt over the side and soon had his arms safely clenched in her talons. With darkness falling, they descended deeper and deeper to the craggy bottom and after their target. It wouldn't be an easy thing to find even with her keen eyesight.

The remaining three warriors turned to the southwest and moved off quickly to try to find Spade's hideout. Above them, a blanket of stars by the thousands slowly materialized in the night sky.

CHAPTER 10

As evening set on Spade's work site, he made a quick estimation on when the apparatus would be fully operational. It was a rather extensive and complicated system — each element relying on the next and then the entire thing had to be connected with interweaving cables, hoses and linkages. He had studied the blueprints dozens of times and nearly had it memorized, but he liked to double-check his work against the plans Axxes had given him just to be sure. His boss had zero tolerance for mistakes and dealt harshly with failure. Burt was confident everything was set up correctly so far; he just wanted to be sure.

Spade wandered back to his 4x4 where he had set down his briefcase before switching to his claw-arm again. He had made sure to lock it inside, just in case those pesky animals tried to come back for it.

He figured he would sleep better knowing that the installation of the bio-lab was on track and, besides, he could finish his sandwich that he had only gotten to take one bite out of. His stomach was grumbling a bit.

Using his key fob to unlock the doors, he turned on

the overhead light and spun the briefcase around so the latches were to the front. With two quick flips of the brass clamps, his leather attaché popped open. He stared into the briefcase dumbfounded. He couldn't believe his eyes.

Most of the file folders, papers, CDs and map were gone, replaced by an assortment of evergreen branches. On top, all that remained of his sandwich was an uneaten section of the crust.

His angry roar echoed across the mountain valley and startled every living thing within a mile of his enraged outburst.

Spade slammed his metal arm against his truck and put a sizable dent in the roof. "No! No! No!" he screamed as he hammered away again on his once pristine Hummer.

*****

With the threat of imminent danger gone, Mesquite, Sequoia and Juniper reverted to their youthful, smaller versions. The walk back toward Spade's camp was difficult in the darkness, but at least it was almost completely downhill since his site was at a much lower elevation.

They stayed on the road for most of their hike, headed in the same direction they last saw the truck driven by the Soldierjacks. Tired and weary after two miles of trotting along, they veered off into a high meadow sprinkled with evergreens and found a safe place to sleep.

Aspen and Cedar had also changed back to their younger selves after scouring around in the dark along the base of the mountain for nearly an hour. They had found only one scrap of paper that must have blown out of the box during its freefall. They decided to hunker down for the night in a natural cove under a massive rock and resume the search at first light.

That same evening, Miranda and her assistants arrived in Grand Lake. She decided to stay in the best hotel in town and set up her operational base from the suite she was renting. Demanding privacy, she paid for every room on the entire floor. Miranda thought she would touch base with Spade in the morning and make sure he was on schedule. After settling in, she sent Nathan an email and got approval of her proposal.

In his bed back in California, Nathan Axxes could hardly sleep. He was giddy with excitement. After months and months of research and testing, planning and plotting, his grandiose scheme was about to

become reality. He had little fear that anyone or anything could stop him now.

*****

Morning came as the intense yellow rays of the sun cracked over the horizon to the east. From their position on the western slope of the Rocky Mountains, Mesquite, Sequoia and Juniper awoke to a gradual lightening of the sky — the sun was still completely blocked by the jagged ridgeline behind them that rose as high as 14,000 feet above sea level.

Stretching and yawning, the three animal friends shook off their sleep. With hardly a word spoken, they were off again on the hunt for Spade's base. They knew they were close.

In the valley floor two miles away and a half mile below, Cedar and Aspen were up and moving as well. Despite being summer, a cool morning mist hovered in the mountainous terrain and Cedar was thankful once again for the thick, bristly coat of hair he was born with.

Aspen, however, shivered and could hardly wait for the warm sun to crest the mountains so she could feel its warm light on her wings and back. But she ignored her discomfort and took to flight anyway, in hopes of

retrieving the lost affirmations of Spade's sinister laboratory in the mountain forest.

As the minutes ticked by, the light grew stronger and soon their visibility was excellent. Almost immediately, Aspen found two more pieces of paper from the briefcase as well as fragments of a CD that had shattered as it impacted on the rocks.

Cedar was scuttling all around, searching along the valley floor and jumping from rock to rock. He also found another document and he held it in his mouth as he continued his hunt.

"I found it!" Aspen cried out. "Cedar! Over here!"

The little black and white badger hurried over to where she was circling and the two of them approached the large hunk of bashed metal that she had spotted with great excitement.

"Finally!" Cedar said after spitting out the paper he was holding in his jaws.

As they got closer and peered inside the folds of metal they realized they were looking at the first container the Soldierjacks had thrown off the cliff. It was void of anything whatsoever.

"Wrong one, huh?" Aspen said, already knowing the answer.

"Yeah, but good eye spotting it," Cedar said. He just

wanted to find it and hurry back to his friends. That climb alone he knew would take him all day, but he couldn't wait to tear into Spade and his robot men. "Let's keep looking. It can't be far."

Back up on the mountain, the little gray wolf, grizzly bear and black-footed ferret were winding their way through a meadow that was blooming with lush grasses and wildflowers. Thick winter snows had finally melted and left a moist, fertile bed for plants to grow. Saplings were again reaching for the sky now that the snowdrifts had released them from their heavy white blanket.

They came to a stream, flowing fast with mountain runoff. All three of them leaned in and lapped up mouthfuls of the icy cold water. It was about three feet across, and a healthy jump for such small critters.

"Think we can make it?" Mesquite questioned the others, but he figured he would jump it no matter what they said.

"I doubt it," Juniper said. "And don't you try it either."

"It's not that far, and it's not that deep," Mesquite said. He was pacing along its bank and looking for the best place to make his leap.

"Even if y-y-you and I can get across," Sequoia said to Mesquite sternly, "Juniper's legs are j-j-just too short and I don't th-th-think she can swim it either."

"I definitely am not swimming across that river," she said defiantly, worried about being swept away. Then she leaned back on her hind legs and crossed her arms to emphasize her objection. "No way."

Mesquite ignored their words and stepped back a few paces from the stream's edge. He lowered his front and raised his rump and tensed his muscles, ready to rush. Then he took off running at full speed and leapt across the creek. He cleared it completely except for his left rear foot that landed with a splash in the frigid water.

"See? Told you I could do it!" Mesquite bragged as he shook the water off his back leg by kicking it out behind him. "Now you guys try."

Juniper looked at Sequoia with pleading eyes. She didn't want him to leave her. Sequoia saw her look of fear and motioned with his big, round head for her to follow him. He sauntered a few yards upstream where a young, six-foot-tall aspen was growing along the riverbank.

"I'll b-b-bend it over and then you cross it like a b-b-bridge," Sequoia said with an assuring smile. Then he stood up on his hind legs and bent the little tree over. The top of it just barely touched the grass on the other side.

Without hesitation, Juniper scrambled up the sapling arched across the stream and in two bounds she was on the other side, safe and dry.

"Chicken," Mesquite said.

"Idiot," she replied.

Sequoia let go of the little tree and it snapped back into place, losing a couple of leaves in the process. Then the helpful bear cub turned uphill a ways and, with a determined look on his face, rumbled down at the watery obstacle and vaulted across it himself.

"She could have made it," Mesquite said, but with little confidence in his voice. "Anyways, good thinking, Sequoia."

For the next 15 minutes, the threesome made their way through the meadow and into a thick cluster of pines. Guided by Sequoia's discerning sense of smell and Mesquite's acute hearing, they picked up on what could only be Spade's encampment.

As they neared the outer perimeter, no doubt guarded by sensors and Soldierjacks alike, they slowed their pace and moved with extreme caution. Finding a large rock amongst the evergreens, the trio decided it was the perfect place to watch Spade and his goons as they continued building their contraption over 200 yards away.

Meanwhile, Cedar and Aspen were growing tired rather quickly. It was baffling to them where the container could be that was thrown off the mountainside.

"I'm going to circle up higher!" Aspen shouted down to her badger pal who had stopped to take a drink from a puddle he came across.

The diminutive peregrine falcon banked from her flight pattern and angled upward. With a few flaps of her wings, she soon gained an extra 100 feet in altitude. Then she resumed flying in a circular pattern and looking amongst the thousands of cracks and crevices that surrounded them on all sides.

"Bingo!" she shrieked. "I found it for sure this time!"

In a few moments, Cedar was by her side and admiring the demolished wreck that was once an empty metal box the size of a stove. It now looked more like a soda can that had been tossed out on a busy highway.

"I can see stuff inside," Aspen said as she stood on a rock and bent her head to look inside the flattened container. "But the metal is all smushed around it."

"That's why I'm here," Cedar proudly said. "Badgers are like can openers with hair!"

Cedar set about ripping and scratching his way into the wreckage. Even as a cub, he was relentless when it came to using his claws. After a few minutes, with just

his little badger rump sticking out, Cedar backed up to reveal a mouthful of papers.

"Awesome!" Aspen shouted.

"Hold on! There's more!" he proclaimed and then squirmed back inside. He came out with another collection of items including the map to Spade's lair and a CD that had somehow stayed intact through the whole crash.

"Okay," Aspen said, flush with excitement. "We got what we came after. Let's get as much as we can carry to the ranger station and then find the others!"

"There's Spade!" Juniper half-shouted to Mesquite and Sequoia as they spied on him through the stand of lodgepole pines that separated them from the enemy camp. The sun had been up for almost an hour.

He had emerged from his trailer and was issuing orders to several Soldierjacks who were standing around awaiting direction. Spade usually slept at the work sites he was supervising, typically on an oversized cot he would set up in the trailer, but sometimes he would pitch a tent. He always removed his artificial arm to sleep — it was just too cumbersome and the cold, hard steel wasn't very nice to curl up next to.

He didn't much care for hotels or motels either. Spade wasn't very personable and, while he was used to people staring at his mechanical limbs, he always despised their whispers and pointing fingers. He was sick of disabled veterans who tried to relate by inquiring if he had lost his arm in the war and annoyed when little kids would ask stupid questions or simply cower at the sight of him.

The animal trio watched from a distance and

noticed very little activity compared to just last night. Hardly a sound emanated from the camp. Either something was stalling the final construction or the lab was finished and running silently.

Spade sent the group of drones that had gathered around him into the woods to join the sentries that were already positioned there. Then he opened the hatch to his shiny black SUV and attached his claw arm. Closing the tailgate, he then climbed into the driver's seat of his 4x4 and drove slowly out of his secret location toward the paved road.

Unbeknownst to the animals watching him, Spade was headed into town to meet with Miranda Wright in her hotel suite. It was a get-together over breakfast where he would bring her up to speed on his progress and they could coordinate each other's efforts. He did not want her to worry and he didn't need her snooping around his work site. Spade didn't trust her at all.

He didn't question her alliance. Miranda was absolutely faithful to Axxes, but Burt considered her a conniving trickster who would love to take over Spade's field operations and make herself that much more powerful. Spade thought of himself as a general in the Axxes army and no woman, especially Miranda, could ever take that away from him.

He was also hoping she could make him a copy of the schematics that were stolen from his briefcase since she most certainly had the same files in her possession. He figured he would just lie to her and tell her that one of the Soldierjacks accidentally corrupted his computer system. That would help explain why he shot a spike through the chest of one of the multimillion-dollar machines.

Miranda had gotten up early, as she usually does. Every morning, she spends an hour in a meditative state while performing seemingly impossible techniques that blend ancient yoga with kung fu.

Afterwards, she typically spars with her assistants who themselves must be black-belt martial artists before they can even join her team. With only two assistants to practice against, she tried to make it more challenging by allowing them to use hand-held weapons. As always, she defeated them in all four combative sessions held in the grass behind the hotel.

"Well, what *do* you guys want to do, now that Spade is gone?" Mesquite asked, itching to get closer.

"We w-w-wait," Sequoia stuttered. "The plan was to wait for the others un-un-unless it looks like they're ready to launch the v-v-virus."

Juniper scowled at her wolf-pup friend. "It was your idea, genius," she added.

Mesquite started to fidget. "Well, how do we know that the thing's not already up and running? We're too far away to tell anything from here."

"Well, for one, I've n-n-never known of a machine made by the humans that d-d-didn't make even a little noise," Sequoia said as he tried to justify not risking being detected.

Mesquite thought about it for a minute. "Okay," he finally said, "I'll give you that, but don't you think we should be over on the other side where we can see the thing he's building by the river? That's the only way we can tell right away if they got it working for sure."

Sequoia and Juniper looked at each and seemed to agree. "Alright," Juniper said, "but we do it slow and smart and we don't get caught."

The little wolf smiled.

"Yeah, Mesquite," Sequoia stressed. "N-n-not like every other time you try to be sneaky. We st-st-stay at a safe distance and we d-d-don't get caught."

"And we wait for the others," Juniper emphasized.

"Okay, already," Mesquite said annoyed at his friends lack of adventure. "We won't get caught. We're animals of the forest, remember? Stealth is what we do. Now follow me!"

Juniper sighed and looked at her bear cub partner.

"That's what I'm worried about — following him!"

In single file, the furry friends wound their way around the encampment and kept hidden amongst the underbrush and rocky landscape. After slogging through a particularly wet area, they had managed to move almost a mile around the outskirts of the site in less than an hour. They could hear the rushing waters of the river just a few feet away. They were much closer now, but the sound overwhelmed their ability to listen. From here, they would have to rely on sight alone.

Sequoia poked his head above the tall wild grass in front of them.

"Can you see anything?" Mesquite asked.

"Not really," the bear said. "They g-g-got camouflage nets up. It's hard to s-s-see anything at all."

"Maybe you should go up a tree," Juniper suggested. Sequoia was a pretty good tree climber.

Mesquite liked her idea, but he wanted to see for himself. "We need to move a little closer," he whispered. "We got to find a spot where we can see the river and their lab at the same time."

"I don't think we should move any closer," Juniper maintained.

"We're still a long ways off from their hideout," Mesquite said. "Let's just go a little closer and then I

promise we'll stop. We're almost there...I just know it."

Sequoia wasn't so sure. "Wait for m-m-me to climb a tree and take a look around first," he proposed.

"There's no time," Mesquite said and then he started moving forward. "Come on!"

After just a few steps, he crossed through an invisible light beam and tripped the perimeter alarm. Soldierjacks sprang into action, several of them converging on the very spot where Mesquite, Sequoia and Juniper crouched. They didn't hear them coming until it was too late.

"Zzt! Intruder alert! Intruder alert!" the robots emanated together like linked loudspeakers. Their warning echoed through the forest and seemed to come from all directions.

"Run!" Mesquite yelled as he turned and bolted from the oncoming androids.

The threesome scrambled in a panic, retreating backwards and fleeing from the red and black menace that surged after them. But there was nowhere to go. The Soldierjacks, waving their deadly Flamesaws, outflanked them and cut off their escape route.

The critters tripped over each other as they sought refuge in an open path that would lead them to safety. After a desperate and unsuccessful few moments of

shear terror, they found themselves backed up to the river's edge. Across the river, four more Soldierjacks arrived. The trio was completely surrounded.

"Zzt! Engage and destroy," came the unified order amongst the armed machine-men.

"My thoughts exactly!" Mesquite shouted to his teammates.

Three blue-green exploding suns radiating from the little animals temporarily blinded the Soldierjacks as they magically morphed into their super-powered alter egos. In seconds, they went from being on the defense to going on the offense.

Juniper took off in a blur, a turquoise-colored streak in her wake, and engaged a pair of Soldierjacks with a series of high-speed kicks and punches that dropped them to their knees and eventually out of commission.

Mesquite brandished his mystical seven-foot-long spear like a bo staff and instantly went to work using it like a well-trained martial artist. Forceful thrusts and strikes quickly toppled any Soldierjacks who got too close to the man-wolf and his punishing fighting style.

Sequoia, now a hulking beast that looked half-man, half-grizzly, used his massive fists to pummel the robots that came within his reach. Armed with an

unbreakable shield that appears whenever he trans-
forms, he used it to deflect torrents of fire that the
Soldierjacks unleashed from their Flamesaws.

Caught unprepared, the Soldierjacks soon realized
the tide of battle was clearly shifting in favor of the
animal heroes. The forest rang out with the sound of
combat as more robots poured in to fight against
their otherworldly foe with seemingly impossible powers.

The giant grizzly crushed a Soldierjack with a horrendous blow from his shield and then picked up the
damaged android and whipped it at two others,
destroying them as well.

Two more of the robot-men jumped on Sequoia's arm
to subdue him, but found that even with their combined strength he was too strong. He hoisted them off
their feet, threw them to the ground and then
stomped on them until they stopped moving.

Still hurtling almost too fast to be seen, Juniper
had drawn her arcane hatchets from the satchel on
her back. Racing in and out of the slower-moving
Soldierjack formations, she buried the brightly glowing
turquoise hatchet heads into the legs and torsos of
the robots, chopping them down like metal trees. They
haphazardly fired away at the ferret-warrior with their
weapons, but could never hit their target.

As a super-powered wolf, Mesquite was difficult to fight. With incredible speed and dexterity, he spun his lance all around him, smacking his combatants with brutal blows that often were enough to disable them.

In the heat of battle, he noticed a Soldierjack had maneuvered behind Sequoia and was about to rip into the brawling bear with the spinning blade of its Flamesaw. With his right hand, Mesquite lifted his spear over his shoulder and hurled it at the cyborg. The gleaming turquoise spear tip rammed into the robot's back and burst out of its chest. As it fell to the ground, Sequoia turned to see what happened and gave his pal an approving wink.

Mesquite dropped a Soldierjack in front of him with a lethal roundhouse kick to the head that nearly decapitated it. Then he ran over to retrieve his spear embedded in the hapless victim.

Soldierjack bodies littered the ground. Some lay motionless, others quivered on the ground, immobilized. Many of them spewed sparks from gaping holes or horrible gashes carved into them by the heroic trio.

Mesquite was having a tough time pulling his spear out of the Soldierjack he had taken out with his well-placed throw. He put one foot on the robot's head as he yanked and pulled on it.

Just as it tore loose, an unexpected, powerful blast struck Mesquite in the back. The mighty wolf fell to his knees and collapsed in the dirt, twitching.

Spade had arrived. He stepped out from a copse of trees and grinned at his fallen foe. A wicked-looking electro-cannon was now serving as his right arm. Smoke wisped out of the peculiar pulsating barrel.

"Mesquite!" Sequoia yelled. Roaring, he charged at Spade with his shield held high in front of him.

Spade fired again but was shocked to see the burst get absorbed harmlessly into the glowing turquoise shapes that surrounded Sequoia's spirit-shield. The giant grizzly was almost on him.

Spade fell to the ground and fired again, this time under Sequoia's shield and directly at his feet. It worked. Unable to deflect the shot in time, the massive bear took the full brunt of the electroshock and it dropped him instantly. With a huge crash, Sequoia fell face first into the dirt, paralyzed.

From across the battlefield, Juniper saw Mesquite and Sequoia go down. She launched into a high-speed attack against Spade.

He saw her racing at him out of the corner of his eye and defensively swung up his mechanical arm to protect himself just in time. Her hatchets cut deep into his

weaponized appendage like cleavers. Juniper had unexpectedly severed the components and electrical lines inside Spade's arm. She was instantly electrocuted and thrown back several feet. She landed in an unconscious heap, not far from Mesquite.

Spade rolled over and quickly disconnected the damaged electro-cannon from his person. He left it on the ground where it fell, spitting sparks and crackling with escaping energy.

Exasperated, he stood. Spade couldn't believe what was happening. A few of the remaining Soldierjacks approached and awaited their orders.

Spade paused; he needed to collect his thoughts. The three strange warriors had defeated well over half of his legion he had stationed with him. He ordered the return of the two nearest Crabtanks as well as twenty more androids. That should give him enough protection from any inquisitive park rangers or police.

He also needed to get the virus lab up and running. Miranda gave him the extra files he needed, so the system should be operational in just a few more hours.

Spade then commanded his Soldierjacks to put the three animal-attackers together, tie each of them in chains and guard them as he went back to his 4x4.

Once there, Spade opened the tailgate and pulled

out his case of arms. Lifting the lid, he removed his beloved spike-shooting cannon from its channel cut in the foam. He snapped it into place on his empty right shoulder and then slapped in a fresh 12-round magazine of the deadly eight-inch-long square nails. But for the dirty little job he had in mind, he knew he would only need three.

Before leaving his SUV, Spade opened his briefcase and took out the CD Miranda had given him. He wanted to make sure the installation of the biotech equipment was back on schedule.

He had halted production the night before when he found out his schematics had been stolen. He knew he was behind, despite telling Miranda just the opposite that morning over coffee.

Spade called to the nearest Soldierjack. "Number 44!" As the worker drone came close, Spade continued giving orders, "Take this data disc inside and bring up the bio-lab blueprints. Confirm that everything is correct with our install and then continue until you got it up and running."

"Zzt! Affirmative," the android replied and then went inside the trailer to carry out his mission.

Behind him, Spade heard a noise. Startled, he turned and saw the two recalled Crabtanks trudging through the woods like iron-skinned leviathans.

He smiled and headed back to his supernatural captives.

Mesquite, Sequoia and Juniper were just starting

to regain consciousness, moaning and blinking their eyes. They were chained tightly and surrounded by six Soldierjacks that kept their Flamesaws aimed, level and ready.

Spade walked up and stood looking down at them, his expression both smug and bewildered.

He was contemplating using them as test subjects for the first batch of infected water the bio-lab was about to produce. It fascinated him to think of having these creatures under his command, to do with as he pleased…real flesh and blood followers whose minds were his to control instead of just an endless supply of robot drones.

As he watched over his prisoners, one of the Crabtanks rumbled up next to him and stopped. The turbo-diesel engine inside its steel hull hissed as the wastegate let off extra exhaust pressure and then settled into a steady, guttural idle. It gave him an idea.

Spade decided to forgo his plans to try to control their minds. These were dangerous animals and he didn't know what they were capable of. Besides, if Axxes knew about it, he would just take them from him or simply order them destroyed. He decided that he could still have his way with them and get his revenge at the same time.

Spade turned to the Crabtank and knocked on the turret with his fist. A Soldierjack inside opened the hatch and stuck its head out.

"Listen up, drone!" Spade ordered. "I want you to take these creatures, one at a time, and treat them like a tree you're about to cut down in the forest."

"Zzt! Affirmative," the mindless Soldierjack answered.

Before it ducked back inside and closed the hatch, Spade shouted out one more order, "Do it nice and slow!"

Spade laughed out loud and stepped back to watch the carnage with a wicked grin.

The engine of the Crabtank fired up as it swiveled its pincer-arm into position over the helpless captors and then engaged the giant spinning blade on the other arm.

The machine reached out and clamped down on Sequoia like a massive set of pliers. The enormous grizzly squirmed in its hydraulic steel claw, but was still too weak to break free. His friends watched in horror as the armored vehicle slowly brought around its saw blade, aimed right at Sequoia's midsection.

Suddenly, the deafening sound of metal being torn asunder pierced the air around them. The Crabtank shuddered violently as if it was exploding from the

inside. Horrendous noise resonated from its very core.

In an instant, it stopped moving altogether. An eerie silence filled the air.

Spade watched in disbelief as the hatch was thrown open and a humanistic badger warrior leaped out and stood with an evil grin of its own on top of the sabotaged tank. Smoke poured out from the hatch opening. The badger-man's claws were like bright blue-green butcher knives.

"Cedar!" Sequoia exclaimed.

The badger smiled back at his friend still clinched in the giant claw of the Crabtank. "Who said you could start this party without me?" he quipped.

"Destroy them! Destroy them all!" Spade screamed and raised his arm to fire.

Just as he did, a sudden unseen force slammed against his back and sent him sprawling face first into the dirt. The spike shot past Cedar's head, missing him by less than inch.

"Thanks, Aspen," Cedar shouted to his teammate who had just streaked down from the clouds and put Spade in the dirt.

The Soldierjacks opened fire with their Flamesaws. Streams of intense fire filled the air as they tried to burn the newly arrived warriors.

Cedar flipped backwards off the tank, landed feet-first on the other side and then spun around to cut a surprised Soldierjack in half.

Aspen ducked as a fiery blast from a nearby Flamesaw shot overhead. She turned, whipped her left wing and launched three turquoise-colored feathers directly at the Soldierjack who attacked her. Her energy-laden quills exploded against the robot like small grenades, knocking it off its feet and out of the fight.

Then she squatted and took off vertically with great force just as three more scorching salvos cooked the space she had just occupied. From the air, she sent more of her explosive feathers screaming down with deadly accuracy and dispatched three more Soldierjacks.

Several of the armed robots ran around the crippled Crabtank to catch the badger warrior in a blistering crossfire. All they found was one of their own cut in half and a freshly dug, large hole in the ground.

To their rear, Cedar burst through the rocky earth right next to Mesquite and Juniper who were struggling to break from their manacles. With one swipe from his claws, the chains gave way and his fellow wolf and ferret warriors joined the fray.

Sequoia, still dangling from the grip of the Crabtank,

surged back to full-strength with an ear-splitting roar. He heaved his arms upward and outward and burst free from the steely grip of the machine's giant claw as well as his chains. The grizzly landed with his feet spread wide and a furious look on his face.

Spade scrambled for cover underneath the Crabtank as chaos erupted all around him.

The super-powered animals were unleashing a terrible fury on the Soldierjack army. Aspen fired never-ending barrages of her detonating feather-missiles from above like neon-blue meteorites, while Cedar tore with reckless abandon through their forces with ferocious, snarling savagery. Mesquite pummeled his aggressors using disciplined, fluid punches and kicks coupled with vicious strikes and jabs from his spear. Juniper brought her own fast-moving storm of hatchet chops and blows, pinging off one Soldierjack to the next like a turbulent pinball gone astray.

Sequoia had seen Spade crawl under the Crabtank and wasn't going to let him escape. With unimaginable brute force, the super-bear swatted a Soldierjack who had gotten too close with his mighty shield and sent the flattened robot flying across the forest. Then he stepped up next to the Crabtank and began smashing his fists down on it. The hull sang out with an awful

sound as Sequoia's blows hammered the tracked vehicle into scrap metal.

With his ears ringing, Spade clamored out from under the tank as it collapsed around him. He got up on one knee, leveled his arm-cannon at the riled grizzly and emptied his magazine at him. The spikes glanced off Sequoia's trusty shield like they were made of plastic.

"What are you creatures?" Spade shrieked and took off running toward his 4x4.

From behind, the second Crabtank came barreling down at Sequoia, but the bear sensed it and swung his shield around just as the immense circular saw blade struck. Sparks arced into the sky as the metal blade sheared away against the unbreakable shield.

Sequoia maneuvered around, away from the dangerous arms of the Crabtank. The robot pilot traversed the treads and the tank shifted sharply, rotating fast.

But Sequoia was ready. He had positioned himself at the back of the armored crawler and with one powerful motion lifted it up, off its still-spinning tracks, and flipped it over on its side.

Mayhem and destruction swirled around the battle zone for a few more minutes until, finally, the last of the Soldierjacks fell to the ground – Mesquite's spear lodged in its head.

The sudden sound of an engine racing disrupted the stillness that had just settled over the forest. Spade slammed his SUV into gear and was speeding away.

"I don't think so," Juniper said, smiling, and then sped off after him. In seconds, she had overtaken the 4x4. She pulled a hatchet out, leaped up onto the hood, and smashed it right into the windshield.

Spade screamed and covered his eyes as his truck turned sharply and smashed into a tree. Juniper had already leaped off and landed safely.

The driver's door flew open and Spade staggered out. Sweat and shards of glass covered his anguished face. He was screaming wildly.

With his nail-gun arm reloaded and set to fire rivets, Spade unleashed a volley of the super-heated bolts at Juniper as he ran for the safety of his trailer. Jumping and twisting her body around like a snake, she managed to just barely dodge the stream of orange-glowing rivets he shot at her.

Spade burst through the door of his trailer, slammed it shut behind him, and locked it. He was panting and sweating profusely.

He knew that the animals had surrounded his trailer. He could hear them and see their shadows from the window and under the door. "You'll never take me alive!"

he shouted, not sure and not caring if they could understand him.

To show he meant business, and hoping he might hit one of the creatures that had attacked his camp, he aimed his arm at the far wall and fired another burst of molten-hot rivets. They punched through the walls of his trailer like stabbing a pencil through paper.

"If you even come close, you savages, I'll pump you full of holes!" he hollered out from inside his aluminum refuge.

He was trying not to panic. Spade crawled over to his desk and fumbled at his keyboard. He needed reinforcements. He needed to call Axxes.

Without warning, the floor to the trailer suddenly tore open. Spade fell back as the angry badger-warrior jumped out of the ruptured hole and pounced on him.

From outside the trailer, Cedar's teammates heard Spade scream and then one last barrage of rivets tore through the roof. All went quiet.

In a few seconds, the trailer door opened and Cedar stepped out, wiping his hands.

"What happened to Spade?" Mesquite asked.

Cedar looked at his friends and, with a wink and a grin, replied, "Oh, I guess you could say I disarmed him."

EPILOGUE

Miranda Wright and her assistants arrived at the devastated work site just minutes after a long line of police and park ranger vehicles came speeding up with their sirens wailing.

They found the bio-lab had been demolished completely and every Soldierjack in the area was destroyed. They discovered Burt Spade in his trailer with his mechanical arm horribly ripped from his body. He was a blubbering, incoherent mess and skittish as a squirrel.

Miranda called Nathan Axxes seeking guidance and he had her immediately follow Spade to the hospital, playing the role of a concerned employer. Burt was the only witness to the true purpose of the work site so, to keep him from talking, he had Miranda give him a special bottle of water and then hand him the phone. Axxes wiped his memories with a special code downloaded into his brain.

With some amazing trickery and clever deception over the next several months, Miranda, representing the Axxes Conglomeration, was able to convince investigators

that the true purpose of the bio-lab was to try to control the minds of fish affected by Whirling Disease. Their experiment in the mountains, she proposed, could have counteracted the terrible brain infection caused by the parasitic affliction that makes river trout chase their tails uncontrollably. Mind control of humans, she said, is not just impossible, but something her company would never research nor pursue.

To show good faith and to keep out of further court hearings, the Axxes Conglomeration agreed to spend millions of dollars to study and find a cure for Whirling Disease. Nathan was outraged.

Spooked by all the allegations and investigations, the government cancelled their contracts they had in place with Axxes. Nathan was infuriated.

Axxes hired special inspectors to determine what had happened at Spade's work site. After weeks of scouring over evidence, they theorized that either it was attacked by a family of large, rabid predators or by a clever, competing corporation who made it look that way. Nathan was incensed. He had to be medicated.

*****

A short time later, on a peaceful and calm summer evening, the Natural Forces team, in their youthful forms, sat on a grassy hill in Rocky Mountain National Park. Crickets happily chirped away in the distance and an owl occasionally called out from a tree not too distant.

On the horizon, the lights of a sleepy tourist town were twinkling. The full moon hung low over the valley and the sky was clear.

"So, where does everyone think we'll go to next?" Aspen asked the others from her perch on a twig.

"I th-th-think we should just stay here," Sequoia said. He knew all of them loved this giant preserve in the mountains and could stay there forever if they could.

"I don't know," Juniper said. "I hear California is nice."

"California?" Cedar grimaced. "I don't want to go to California."

"Then maybe Oregon?" she offered.

"We go where we're guided to go, guys," Mesquite reminded them. "Like always."

From their places on the hilltop, Aspen, Cedar and Juniper all mumbled simultaneously in agreement.

Sequoia huffed. "It'd sure be nice if the spirits guided us toward food for once," Sequoia said, which brought a heartfelt burst of laughter from the whole group that echoed out long into the night.

DON'T MISS OUT!

It's predator against prey in the Northwoods of Minnesota once Colonel Shaka sets his sights on the Natural Forces!